Welcome to *Where?*

Book
1

Grosset & Dunlap

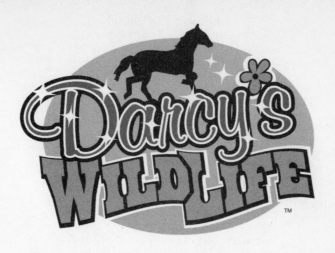

Welcome to *Where?*

Book 1

By Jory Simms

Based on a teleplay
written by Doug Tuber and Tim Maile

A Stan Rogow Book • Grosset & Dunlap

GROSSET & DUNLAP
Published by the Penguin Group
Penguin Group (USA) Inc., 375 Hudson Street, New York, New York 10014, U.S.A.
Penguin Group (Canada), 10 Alcorn Avenue, Toronto, Ontario, Canada M4V 3B2
(a division of Pearson Penguin Canada Inc.)
Penguin Books Ltd, 80 Strand, London WC2R 0RL, England
Penguin Ireland, 25 St Stephen's Green, Dublin 2, Ireland
(a division of Penguin Books Ltd)
Penguin Group (Australia), 250 Camberwell Road, Camberwell, Victoria 3124,
Australia (a division of Pearson Australia Group Pty Ltd)
Penguin Books India Pvt Ltd, 11 Community Centre, Panchsheel Park,
New Delhi - 110 017, India
Penguin Group (NZ), Cnr Airborne and Rosedale Roads, Albany, Auckland 1310,
New Zealand (a division of Pearson New Zealand Ltd)
Penguin Books (South Africa) (Pty) Ltd, 24 Sturdee Avenue, Rosebank, Johannesburg
2196, South Africa

Penguin Books Ltd, Registered Offices:
80 Strand, London WC2R 0RL, England

Text copyright © 2005 Stan Rogow Productions (U.S.),
© 2005 Temple Street Releasing Limited (Canada).
Series and logo copyright © 2005 Darcy Productions Limited,
a subsidiary of Temple Street Productions Limited.
DISCOVERY KIDS, DISCOVERY and all related indicia are
trademarks of Discovery Communications, Inc., used under license.
All rights reserved. DiscoveryKids.com

Published by Grosset & Dunlap, a division of Penguin Young Readers Group,
345 Hudson Street, New York, New York 10014.
GROSSET & DUNLAP is a trademark of Penguin Group (USA) Inc.
Printed in the U.S.A.

Library of Congress Control Number: 2005011423

ISBN 0-448-43987-5   10 9 8 7 6 5 4 3 2

Hi!

I'm Sara, and I play Darcy Fields on <u>Darcy's Wild Life</u>. I'm so excited to be writing to you!

On <u>Darcy's Wild Life</u>, Darcy is the daughter of a movie star, accustomed to premieres, private jets, and partying in style—so, it was quite a shock when her mother decided to leave such a glamorous life for a "normal life" on a farm in the middle of nowhere.

I love Darcy because she is an optimist and so am I. In real life my childhood has been the opposite of Darcy's. I grew up in California with two great parents, and I have only one animal in my home, my pet dog, Jenny.

I've always wanted to be an actress, and it's amazing to see my dreams coming true. In some ways my life may be easier than Darcy's, but the point is that for better or worse, we all find ourselves in situations that are totally unfamiliar or unexpected. Darcy complains, sure, but at heart, she really does her best to get with the program—and she learns a lot about herself in the process. Personally, I think that's a great lesson!

I hope you enjoy my books, and thank you for watching my show.

Best Wishes!

♡ always,

Sara Paxton

✳ (DARCY'S DISH) ✳

Hey, my people. This is my first blog post from the town of Bailey or, as people back home would say, "Where?!" I know, I know. I usually post from my favorite Rodeo Drive e-café or from a sunny table at the Chateau Marmont. Tragically, those days are over. I've moved from my Malibu mansion to a cute but totally location-challenged farmhouse! I couldn't feel more out of place.

"So, Darcy," you might be asking right now, "why the heck did ya move to . . . what was it called? Barley?"

My answer? "Ask my mom!" This move from Hollywood to the heartland was her idea. That's right. It was my mother who wanted to move to the country. My mother, the famous, glamorous, and—let's face it—slightly high-maintenance movie star, Victoria Fields.

Whoops, I keep forgetting—Mom's new title is Former Movie Star.

So, what does that make me? Bummin' in a big way! It seems like only yesterday that life was so different. . . .

Chapter 1

Wild Wisdom . . . *Cows can walk upstairs but not down them because a cow's knees cannot bend properly to walk down stairs.*

It was an average evening in the life of Darcy Fields. Y'know—stepping gracefully out of a white limo into a flurry of popping flashbulbs. Cruising down the red carpet outside a Hollywood theater. Fully intending to swipe some popcorn out of Jude Law's bucket during the movie premiere. The usual.

Yes, it was just an average night, but Darcy wasn't complaining. She *adored* her life. And you could see it on her superglossy smile as she and her mom greeted the first TV reporter of the evening.

"And here's tonight's leading lady, Victoria Fields, along with her fabulous daughter, Darcy," the reporter gushed into her microphone. Darcy smiled graciously and flipped a hank of long, blond hair over her shoulder.

Meanwhile, her mother flashed her most super-superstar smile.

"Hello, you wonderful people," she called to the fans who lined the carpet, screaming in delight. "You're simply wonderful. *Wonderful.*"

Darcy smiled and shook her head affectionately.

There Mom goes again, she thought. *Totally ignoring her showbiz duties to give back to her fans. Looks like I'll have to step in and give this reporter what she's after.*

"Tell us, Victoria," the reporter said, leaning toward the megastar, "what are you—"

"My mom's wearing Sergio Georgini," Darcy announced, gesturing at her mother's sparkly red gown with a flourish that would have made Vanna White proud.

"And," the reporter continued breathlessly, "is it true you—"

"That's right!" Darcy said, expertly anticipating the reporter's next question. (She'd been doing this movie premiere thing all her life, after all!)

"She did all her own stunts," Darcy confirmed.

"And what about—"

"Yes!" Darcy trilled. "She learned to speak Japanese for the movie!"

"*Kochira wa keisatsuda akiramete,*" Victoria demonstrated, her sunny face suddenly going dead-serious. "*Tomarinasai domo arigoto.*"

As the TV reporter jumped backward, Victoria and Darcy winked at each other.

Mom so rocks, Darcy thought proudly. *I mean, not only does she have Japanese totally down, you can't hear a trace of her English accent. If I didn't know better, I'd think she just got off a plane from Tokyo! Whoops, Ms. TV reporter looks confused. Better translate.*

Darcy smiled big, leaned into the microphone, and explained, "That means, 'Freeze, punk!' "

"So, where are you headed after the movie?" the reporter said as more flashbulbs popped and more cheers filled the air.

Ooh, this is the best question yet, Darcy thought.

"Well," Victoria said, giving her own blond curls a flip, "there's the first post-party at Ashton Kutcher's house. He's a dear!"

"Then," Darcy piped up, "there's the second post-party on J Lo's yacht."

"Then we're flying to London for the European premiere of the movie," Victoria added with a tinkly laugh.

"And *then*," Darcy cried, "Paris for the fashion shows."

"You're a busy young lady," the reporter said, her eyebrows raised.

"Well, it's a three-day weekend," Darcy replied with

wide eyes. "I've gotta do *something*."

As the reporter laughed, Darcy and her mother glanced at each other and smiled. They'd nailed another Hollywood moment.

I'm so glad I TiVo'd Entertainment This Evening, Darcy thought. *I love coming home from a premiere with Mom, breaking out the Ben & Jerry's, and watching ourselves on TV. It's classic mother-daughter bonding!*

But the reporter wasn't quite finished.

"Last question, Darcy?"

Darcy nodded and waited with a camera-ready smile.

"Why would your mother give up this incredible life," the woman inquired, "to go live on a ranch in the middle of nowhere?"

Darcy Fields's blood ran so cold, her feet felt like they'd turned to ice. And since this was a typical Hollywood evening—totally warm and balmy—she couldn't blame her strappy sandals.

Ranch? she said to herself. *Middle of nowhere?! That sounds awful!*

"What?!" Darcy said with a rasp. "Why would she do that?"

The reporter looked bewildered. Which was exactly how Darcy felt.

"Why," Darcy repeated desperately, "would she *do* that? Why would she do that? Why would she do—"

"*Moooooo.*"

Darcy gasped and sat up.

In bed.

Yup, she'd been dreaming. She'd been dreaming from her new bedroom, in her new farmhouse, in her new middle-of-nowhere town.

Oh, and one more thing:

There was a *cow* standing over her bed.

As if she needed a reminder that her life had fallen incredibly far from its old, Hollywood splendor, the bovine bogeyman emitted another loud, smelly *moooo*.

Darcy gaped at the farm animal invading her personal space and sighed, "Why did she do that?"

"*Moooo.*"

Darcy scowled, propped herself on her elbows, and gazed out her bedroom window. The view she'd grown up with—the grand homes of Malibu, partially obscured by classic, Southern California smog—was nowhere to be seen. And those twinkling lights? Those weren't paparazzi flashbulbs. They were stars, twinkling down into the silent, *boring* night.

Darcy Fields had a new kind of average night. It was hay-scented, farm-fresh, and megaboring.

The former movie star's daughter flopped back onto her pillow and uttered the question again: "Why?!"

Chapter 2

Wild Wisdom . . . *Ducks never feel cold in their feet, even if they swim in icy cold water.*

As Darcy stumbled down the stairs, still in her pajamas, she felt bleary-eyed. The smell of clean, country air wafting through the open front door was making her nose itch.

Her mother, on the other hand, was in heaven.

She was in heaven even though she was on her hands and knees, *unpacking her own boxes*!

Darcy blinked.

Okay, she thought, *now I've seen it all. My movie-star mom is happily doing manual labor. I know she likes to do her own stunt work, but this is ridiculous.*

"Good morning, my pet," Victoria singsonged, completely oblivious to her daughter's distress. "Aren't you simply in love with the country? Getting up early, chopping wood, wandering through the meadows, seeing the stars in the sky. . . ."

"I want to see stars where they belong—at your movie premieres," Darcy said as she flopped onto the living-room couch. Like everything else in the newly purchased farmhouse, it was cozy and comfy, but not exactly fashion-forward.

"And I don't like chopping," Darcy added. "I like shopping! And I really don't need a cow in my bedroom."

That made Victoria pause. And not much made Victoria Fields pause. As you've probably read in any number of celebrity gossip magazines, she was Eccentric with a capital E. She came by it naturally. Her whole family was famous for being adventurous, free-spirited theater folk (like the Barrymores, but with English accents). And Victoria was the most kooky Fields of all. She liked to dress up in dramatic costumes. She started every day with extremely loud vocal exercises that she'd learned from a Tuvan throat singer on some mountain in Tibet. In short, she was totally comfortable with all things weird.

Duh, Darcy thought. *Why else would she have come up with this out-there idea of moving us to the country?*

So, it was no surprise that Victoria was delighted with the idea of a barnyard animal drooling onto her daughter's duvet.

"How did a cow get in your bedroom?" she asked

with an astonished grin.

"I don't know," Darcy complained. "I just know it was there."

"I suppose it must have come up the stairs," Victoria mused.

Okay, Darcy said to herself, *I know Mom's giddy from all the homegrown vegetables she's been eating, or all the flower pollen in the air or something. But come on! A* cow *in my bedroom? Doesn't that call for a little TLC? Or maybe a first-class ticket back to California?*

"I guess the cow walked up the stairs," Darcy sighed. "My *point* is, I don't—"

"I didn't know cows could climb stairs," Victoria said, putting a manicured finger to her chin. "Isn't that the most charming thing?"

"It's *not* charming, Mom! It's weird," Darcy cried. "I really think leaving Malibu and moving here was a mistake!"

"Well, then you shouldn't have stayed out till four in the morning at Colin Farrell's swimming party," Victoria said, trying for a stern expression (and totally failing). "And you shouldn't have been photographed in Aspen, dancing with the Olympic bobsled team."

"Wait," Darcy sputtered. "I didn't do those things. *You* did."

Victoria put her other finger to her temple and thought hard.

"Ohhh, that's right," she said with a guilty smile. "But Darcy, it was _you_ who hired a helicopter to take you and your friends to Ensenada for churros."

Darcy's indignant face fell. She could not deny it. At the time, going for flyby doughnuts had seemed like the responsible thing to do. After all, Darcy was fourteen, so she couldn't drive yet. And taking a taxi would have been _so_ un-Hollywood, which might have damaged Victoria's sparkly reputation. Right?

Wrong.

"So," Victoria said smugly as she rose to her feet, "that's all the more reason for us to leave that show-biz craziness behind. We're both better off here. Simple values, simple pleasures."

Going back to unpacking mode, Victoria padded over to the fireplace and plunked her Best Actress Oscar on the mantel. Then she plopped a tiny cowboy hat on the poor guy's head.

Darcy shook her own head in wonder. Somehow, Victoria managed to be eccentric and flighty out in the world, but this totally responsible mom at home. Darcy knew she was lucky to have such an über-parent in her life, but she had to admit—sometimes it was darn inconvenient!

At least Victoria hadn't cut *all* non-simple things from their new life. When Darcy spotted her laptop on the coffee table, she pounced on it with a grin.

Ah, she thought to herself, propping the computer on her jammie-clad knees. *My good, old computer. My one and only hookup with my old Hollywood life.*

After opening the laptop, Darcy hit a few buttons to find her way into her weblog. She smiled as Darcy's Dish booted up, complete with funky, retro flowers and pics of all the glam friends she'd left behind.

It was to these faraway buds that Darcy was writing as she blogged:

❋ (DARCY'S DISH) ❋

Hello, my people. So, I'm still in Bailey. And I'm still hoping Mom will change her mind and think about moving back home. There's nothing to get excited about around here.

❋   ❋   ❋   ❋   ❋   ❋

"Oh, look!" Victoria piped up from across the room. "A duck!"

Darcy looked up from her screen to see, indeed, a duck waddling through the front door. It quacked a couple of times and shook its tail feathers. Its webby feet slapped against the hardwood floor.

Like I said, Darcy thought, *there's* nothing *to get excited about here.*

As the duck quacked some more, Victoria began a bubbly conversation with it. "Good morning, Mr. Duck. Or is it Mrs. Duck?"

Needless to say, the duck didn't respond. Darcy rolled her eyes, but her mother was unfazed.

"No matter," Victoria announced. "I shall call you Reginald Winston Alistair van Duck. Or Chuck. Chuck the Duck! I love naming animals."

Darcy sighed heavily.

❋ (**DARCY'S DISH**) ❋

Okay, time for Plan B.

❋   ❋   ❋   ❋   ❋   ❋

Closing her laptop, Darcy made her eyes go wide and sparkly. She'd learned that trick from her mom's romantic comedies.

"Mom," she said brightly. "How can we take care of a whole ranch when we can't even keep the animals out of the house? Guess we have to move back home. . . ."

Darcy concentrated on looking *really* disappointed. Heartbroken, even—until her mother pooh-poohed her idea the way only a mom with an English accent can.

"Don't be silly!" Victoria said. "I hired someone

from the next ranch over to be our handyman. He's in the kitchen now, seeing to breakfast."

"Great," Darcy sighed, opening her laptop back up.

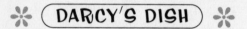

So much for Plan B. My mom hired some local coot to help out around here.

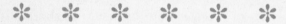

Clannnnggg!
"Oh, man!"

Chapter 3

Wild Wisdom . . . *Sheep hate to be alone—that's why they live in flocks.*

As another *crash*, followed by a wet *splat*, echoed from the kitchen, Darcy jumped to her feet. She hurried across the terra-cotta–tiled dining room with her mom on her heels.

It sounds like the pots are waging war on the pans in there, Darcy thought. *It also sounds like the coot is a klutz!*

When Darcy and Victoria made it to the kitchen, she found a guy sprawled on the floor. His thick brown hair was dusted with flour, his supertan face was smeared with pancake batter, and his bright blue eyes looked guilty.

Did I say local coot? Darcy corrected herself (while wondering how bad her bedhead looked). *I meant local* cute!

"Sorry, Mrs. Fields," the dude said, struggling to

wipe some of the batter off his jeans as he got to his feet. "I ran into a little hitch with the pancakes."

"Eli," Victoria said with a laugh in her voice. "This is my daughter, Darcy."

Eli stumbled over, his hand extended. Darcy smiled as she took it. And then she struggled to keep smiling, despite the fact that Eli had just smeared cold pancake batter all over her palm.

"Hi," the cutie said. "I'm Eli Whitebear. Welcome to Bailey—oh, man!"

He'd just become aware of his battery handshake. After staring for a mortified moment at Darcy's sticky hand, he spun around abruptly.

"Here," he cried, dashing across the kitchen. "Let me get that."

Gallantly, he grabbed a paper towel for Darcy. Unfortunately, when he presented it to her, the towel was still attached to the roll!

So now Eli's also succeeded in creating a paper trail all the way across our kitchen, Darcy thought, giggling. But Eli looked so distressed she added, out loud, "It's okay. This'll work."

Darcy took the superlong towel and cleaned off her hand.

"So," Eli said, "how do you like your eggs?"

Darcy pondered the question for a moment, then

told the truth: "Served by the side of the pool at the Beverly Hills Hotel."

"Um," Eli said, peeking out the kitchen window to the grassy yard. "We don't have a pool."

"Then I'll have scrambled," Darcy sighed.

As Eli made *another* attempt at breakfast—and promptly broke an egg on the counter—another boy arrived. This one was a shrimpy kid with a head full of wild brown hair. He was knocking at the back door, peering hungrily through the window. When Darcy opened the door and said, "Can I help you?" the kid barely looked at her. In fact, he sauntered right past her.

"Yeah, hi, how ya doin'," he said in a raspy, knowing voice. Then he crossed the kitchen to the table, where Victoria was sipping coffee.

"So it's true," the kid crowed. "The famous Victoria Fields, here in Bailey. How cool is that?"

Without any more ceremony, the kid slapped a movie magazine onto Victoria's place mat. The star herself graced the cover.

"Sign that please," the kid requested.

"My pleasure," Victoria said, putting down her coffee cup and taking a fat Magic Marker from the kid. Darcy's mom was totally tolerant of her fans.

"Who am I to make it out to?"

"Jack Adams," the boy blurted. "Say, 'You rock, Jack Adams.' I'm Jack Adams."

"Apparently," Darcy whispered to herself with a giggle, "he's Jack Adams."

As Victoria scrawled on the magazine cover, Jack swiped up her mug.

"Here," he said, sauntering to the coffeepot on the counter and refilling the cup. "Let me heat this up for you. You know, I thought you were great in that movie with that one actor, you know, the one with the hair. . . ."

"Oh, sure," Victoria said with a laugh. "Antonio Banderas. *Look Both Ways*. I learned flamenco dancing for that one. *Olé!*"

Darcy's mom clicked some imaginary castanets above her head.

"That's so great!" Jack grinned—before producing another magazine and plunking it onto the table along with Victoria's coffee cup. "Here, sign this, too."

"And who is this for?" Victoria wondered, uncapping her marker again.

"Make that," Jack said slyly, "to Lucky Winning Bidder."

Oh man, talk about slick, Darcy thought with an eye roll. *This kid is worse than a Hollywood agent.*

Victoria looked just as dubious.

"Hey," Jack said defensively. "A kid's got to make a living."

"I've got a better idea," Victoria teased. She wrote, "You rock, Jack Adams."

"Aw," Jack complained.

"Oh, man!" Eli shrieked from the stove. Darcy, Victoria, and Jack all whirled around and gasped. Eli's eggs were on fire!

And if our local klutz doesn't watch out, his fabu hair is gonna go up in flames, too! Darcy thought in alarm.

Jack wasn't burdened with the same worries. He watched coolly as Eli struggled with the blaze, then stage-whispered to Victoria, "Could you sign a few more mags? I can sell them to the firemen!"

Chapter 4

Wild Wisdom . . . *All horses have two legs on one side of their body that are slightly shorter than the other two.*

She couldn't speak for the singed and chagrined Eli, but for Darcy, the kitchen fire was *so* not a biggie. And why was that?

Because right after the burned breakfast, a very special delivery arrived.

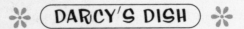

❋ (DARCY'S DISH) ❋

The movers finally delivered my clothes this morning! All my friends—Donna Karan, Emanuel Ungaro, Calvin Klein, my little fabric family. . . .

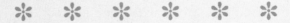

Darcy ran out to the patio, where half a dozen wardrobe boxes were brimming with her filmy dresses. And beautiful sweaters. And kickin' capris. And . . . one very large brown animal with a white stripe on its nose and a distinctly haylike odor.

It was a horse, rummaging through the tallest box. A silky, turquoise blouse was fluttering from the side of its head! It was stuck in its bridle!

"Hey!" Darcy screamed at the equine intruder. "Get out of there!"

The horse flared its nostrils at her rudely, but it did take a few steps backward. And guess what? The blouse went with it.

"That's my Stella McCartney blouse!" Darcy shrieked. She leaped at the horse. "Give me that!"

The horse dodged her neatly. Darcy tried again. The horse shimmied out of her way once more, this time with a whinny that sounded a *lot* like a taunting giggle.

Okay, Darcy told herself. *Everybody knows that a horse's brain is about the size of a walnut. Which means, I simply have to outwit this guy.*

She scanned the grass and saw a chunky branch. Swooping it up, she cooed at the horse.

"Look, I've got a nice stick."

She tossed the stick toward the fence.

"Fetch the stick!" she ordered the horse. "Go get it, boy!"

The horse stood stock-still and stared at Darcy.

Darcy fumed. She snorted with rage. And then, she pounced.

"Give me that," she grunted, trying to yank her blouse out of the horse's filthy bridle. The horse neighed and backed up.

Stella McCartney blouses are known for their delicate beauty, their soft colors, and their romantic lines. They are *not* known for their strength in barnyard battles.

Rrrrippp!

Darcy went tumbling into a big pile of hay, and *half* of her lovely Stella went with her.

"Ooohh!" Darcy growled, spitting out a mouthful of dried grass. She was just lurching to her feet when her mother and Jack emerged from the house.

"Darcy, dear," Victoria said. "What on earth are you doing?"

"I was just missing the wheatgrass juice I used to drink at the spa," Darcy said sarcastically.

"Well, you're ruining your blouse," Victoria said.

"I didn't do it!" Darcy complained, waving the torn top at the horse. "It did!"

The horse lifted its eyebrows.

Oh, yeah, Darcy said to the horse in her mind. *Act all innocent now.*

To add insult to injury, Victoria was looking at the horse with a beaming smile.

"What should we name that horse, Jack?" she

asked her new sidekick. "Darcy, Jack and I are going to name all the animals on the ranch today."

"How about," Darcy proposed, "you name it 'Keep Away from Darcy's Stuff'?"

"Too long," Jack scoffed. "I like Gus."

"Gus it is!" Victoria pronounced. "Would you care to join us, Darcy?"

"Naw," Darcy said. "I was going to go into town and buy things until I feel better."

She made a great effort to wipe the sullen look off her face and replace it with a supersweet one.

"Can I have some money?" she asked her mother, oh-so-charmingly.

"No, no," Victoria trilled. "Simple values. Simple pleasures. You know that."

"I do know that," Darcy said, her shoulders slumping. "I just don't know what that means."

"It means we're going to live like normal people," Victoria said.

Darcy put a finger to her cheek.

"Still not following. . . ."

"We're going to do our own dishes," Victoria said cheerfully. "We're going to make our own beds. If you want things, you're going to have to earn your own money to buy them."

Darcy stifled a gasp. She took a few stumbling

steps toward her mother so she could look deep into her bright blue eyes.

Yup, she looked serious. But still, Darcy *had* to make sure she'd heard Victoria correctly.

"You're saying I have to," she said with a squeak, "wo—wo—work?"

"That's what people do," Victoria declared. "Come along, Jack. Let's go name some sheep."

As her mother and the squirt sauntered off, Darcy stayed riveted to her patch of grass. She couldn't move. She could barely breathe!

"Work?!" she squeaked.

Neeeiiggghh.

Darcy whirled around to glare at Gus, who was definitely mocking her now.

I'm being teased by a horse. On a ranch. In the middle of nowhere.

The thought was terrible enough to give Darcy the strength to move. Glaring at the sassy horse, she grabbed one of her clothes boxes and ran into the house.

An hour later, after she'd changed into her favorite flower-bedecked capris and a little white top with pink trim, Darcy felt a bit better.

But *just* a bit. She began wandering around the

ranch grounds, wondering how on earth she was going to earn some money. In the backyard, she ran into Eli, who had troubles of his own. The board he'd just cut to make a charming little window box for the back of the house was several inches short of the brackets he'd already mounted on the wall.

"Oh, man," Eli complained.

"Eli," Darcy said with a sigh, "I need to earn money."

Eli look grateful for an excuse to ditch his current project. He thought for a moment, then said, "Tell you what. I'm gonna go muck out the stable. You could help, and I'll pay you half of what your mom's paying me."

"Sounds great!" Darcy said with a grin. "Thanks!"

Wow, she thought. *My first job! That wasn't hard at all.*

As she began to follow Eli to the barn, she thought to ask one question.

"So . . . what exactly is 'mucking out stables'?"

Chapter 5

Wild Wisdom . . . *Douglas, Wyoming, has
declared itself to be the jackalope capital of
America, and every year the town hosts
Jackalope Day, usually held in June.*

❋ (DARCY'S DISH) ❋

My people, you don't even want to know what mucking
out stables is! Suffice it to say, it involves a very big shovel
and the, ahem, leavings of a very large horse. The smell
was to die for, and not in a good way. My imported Swiss
potpourri didn't make a dent in it, no matter how much of
the stuff I dumped in Gus's stall. . . .

After what seemed like a laborer's eternity, Darcy
stumbled out of the horse stall, a shovel in one work-
gloved hand and an empty potpourri box in the other.
Just then, her mother and Jack walked into the barn.

"Well," Victoria said crisply. "We've been naming
animals."

"Sounds better than what I'm doing," Darcy grumbled.

"Tragically," Victoria added with a forlorn look at her sidekick, "Jack didn't much like any of the names I came up with."

"No, no," Jack protested. "I *did* like them. They were *great* names. It's just animals in the country don't *respond* to certain names, and those were all the ones you were coming up with."

That duck this morning did *seem to prefer Chuck to Reginald Winston Alistair van Duck*, Darcy had to admit to herself.

"So you see my problem," Victoria said to Darcy.

"It's not a problem," Jack said in his best wheeler-dealer voice. "We'll go out again after lunch. *I'll* come up with some names. You'll pay me fifty cents per name. It'll all be beautiful."

"Wait," Darcy said to her mom. "You're paying *him* to do chores?"

"I'll pay you to do chores, too," Victoria countered. "I've made a list of some animal supplies we need. I'll pay you ten dollars to go to the veterinary clinic and pick them up."

"I'll do it!" Jack piped up. "My dad's the veterinarian!"

"No, *I'll* do it," Darcy insisted. She handed him her

shovel. "*You* help Eli."

As Darcy started out of the barn, she glanced over her shoulder.

See ya later, horse stall, she thought with a relieved sigh. *Bye-bye, Eli! Ooh, and by the way. . . .*

"Watch where you step there, Eli," she warned her former coworker.

Squelch!

Eli looked down at his mucky shoe and held his nose.

"Oh, man," he complained.

Darcy slapped her hand over her mouth and ordered herself not to laugh until she'd made it out of the barn.

A few minutes later, Darcy arrived at the vet. (Don't forget, Bailey was a *really* small town!) It looked more like a Wild West storefront than a vet's office! It had a wooden front porch, a swinging screen door, even a hitching post out front for sick horses. The sign out front said "Creature Comforts."

When Darcy went inside, the place was as empty as a saloon at high noon. The only person there was some grizzled old man, snoozing on a bench beneath the front window. Darcy glanced around at the slightly dusty shelves of mysterious animal products and at the counter with no one standing behind it.

Well, Darcy sighed, *I guess if I was hoping for some action at the veterinary clinic, I came to the wrong place.*

She stepped up to the counter and noticed a sign propped below a stuffed jackalope (which was, of course, a jackrabbit with antelope antlers).

"Press nose," the sign read. "We'll hop right out."

Giggling, Darcy pressed the jackalope's nose. It made a wild squawking noise. It was so funny, Darcy pressed the nose again. And again. And *again.*

"Okay, okay! Where's the fire?"

Darcy jumped as a serious-looking girl with pale skin and an auburn ponytail stormed into the shop from a back room.

"Is this an emergency?" the girl said, finally coming to a halt opposite Darcy. "Where's your animal?"

"No animal," Darcy chirped with a shrug. "Just me."

The girl looked flummoxed for a moment. But then, she looked Darcy up and down, from her sparkly pink eye shadow to her cute, pink slingback shoes.

"Let me guess," the girl said, crossing her arms over the apron she was wearing. "You're that movie star's kid."

"Yeah!" Darcy gushed, delightedly surprised to be

recognized. "Darcy Fields. And you are?"

"Kinda busy right now," the girl said.

Kinda rude, too, Darcy thought. Instantly, she felt dejected. She was not getting off to a good start with this girl. That was disappointing. When Darcy had spotted her storming up to the counter, the first thing she'd thought was, *Bling! Friend material! This girl looks about my age. And unlike Jack and Eli, she's female! There's nothing wrong with being a guy, but let's face it—a guy is just not gonna become your BFF. For that I need a girlfriend!*

But the odds of *this* girl becoming Darcy's Bailey BFF? Definitely slim to none. She barely wanted to give Darcy the time of day. She hadn't even told her her name!

"My dad's delivering a litter of pigs in the back," the girl said curtly.

"Delivering them where?" Darcy asked, blinking. Then she thought for a moment and blurted, "Oh! I get it . . . ew!"

Trying to shake the image of a pig giving birth out of her mind, she thrust her mother's list across the counter.

"Anyway," she said, "my mom needs these supplies."

The girl glanced at the piece of paper, rolled her

eyes, and hollered, "JoJo! We got an order!"

Darcy jumped as a plaid-shirted thug stomped out of the back room, which was obviously the "clinic" part of Creature Comforts Veterinary Clinic. He grabbed Darcy's list with a grunt. As he looked it over, the girl said with a sneer, "Could you get all this together for Miss Beverly Hills, here?"

Grunting again, JoJo stalked into a storeroom, through a door behind the counter.

Whoa, Darcy thought as she heard him begin to clatter around. *That dude is rough. No wonder this girl is so irritable. She's got no one fun to talk to. Maybe she'll give me a chance if I remind her what real girl-talk feels like.*

Darcy smiled sweetly at the girl and said, "Actually, I'm from Malibu. It's a common misconception that all movie people live in Beverly Hills."

"Oh, my," the girl said, her eyes going wide. "I hope I didn't offend you."

Okay, was that comment dripping with sarcasm or is it just me? Darcy thought. But since she didn't see any other friend material lurking about, she decided again to give the girl the benefit of the doubt.

"No offense," Darcy said brightly. "I mean, we *go* to Beverly Hills. Like, if you want to shop at Tiffany's. You should see that place—they have diamonds the size of walnuts."

"Well, here in Bailey," the girl said drily, "we have walnuts the size of walnuts."

"Uh-huh," Darcy replied. "So then, where do people buy jewelry?"

"*If* they buy jewelry, they go to Gilchrist."

Darcy looked at the girl's lobes and wrists with a sinking heart. They were naked—completely platinum-, gold-, and silver-free! Naturally. Could this kid be any more opposite from Darcy, who was decked out in dangly, rhinestone earrings and a tinkling, silver charm bracelet?

"Is Gilchrist a shop in town?" Darcy said with a squeak.

"No," the girl said with exaggerated patience. "It's a city. A few hundred miles from here."

"Oh," Darcy sighed. "So, you probably don't have a day spa, yoga studio, or a tanning salon either, huh?"

"Yet somehow," the girl drawled, "we manage to go on surviving."

"How?" Darcy wailed.

Chapter 6

Wild Wisdom . . . *Pigs cannot sweat because they have no sweat glands. They roll around in the mud to cool their skin.*

Well, at least Darcy had ten dollars to look forward to. Half an hour after she'd arrived at Creature Comforts, JoJo was almost done assembling her order. He'd piled several heavy boxes on the clinic's front porch next to a stack of fifty-pound bags of feed.

The surly girl behind the counter led Darcy out to the front porch to double-check the order. After she'd compared the pile of stuff with Victoria's list, she nodded.

"Thanks, JoJo," she said to the now-sweaty guy. "You can go grab lunch."

JoJo nodded, spat over the porch rail, and skulked off down the street.

Meanwhile, the girl turned to Darcy.

"We'll send a bill out to your place," she said.

"Where's your truck?"

"Um . . ." Laughing nervously, Darcy pointed to her pink bicycle, parked by the hitching post.

I knew *something was wrong with this scenario*, Darcy berated herself. *Out here in the country, you're not supposed get around town on a bike. Or a scooter. Or a Segway. The most I could haul with my vehicle of choice is a bag of lunch!*

"I don't have a truck with me," Darcy admitted.

"So, how were you planning to get this stuff home!" the girl demanded.

Darcy cringed.

"I don't suppose there's anywhere where I could hire a helicopter to haul this?" she joked. When the girl glared at her, she added, "Kidding, of course. I'll have to come back with my mom. Maybe this will fit in her convertible."

"All right," the girl said with a nod. "Take it back in."

"What?!"

Darcy gaped at the giant pile of supplies.

"JoJo's at lunch," the girl said smugly. "You can't leave this sitting here. *Raccoons* will come and eat it."

Darcy shuddered, which seemed to be exactly the reaction the girl was going for. She laughed lightly, then traipsed back into Creature Comforts.

Gingerly, Darcy grabbed a corner of a feed bag and began dragging it across the porch.

I never thought I'd think such a thing, she grunted to herself, *but I wish JoJo were here!*

Jack swiped at his brow. Despite the afternoon's balmy weather, it was sweaty and clammy. Jack felt a little queasy, too. He couldn't help it. He was working harder than he'd ever worked before.

He propped his chin on the fence and thought hard. Finally, he declared, "I've got it! Dwight!"

Then he addressed the sheep he'd been pondering directly. "You'll be Dwight."

He held his breath and looked up at Victoria, who was standing next to him in the sheep corral. She grinned and nodded firmly.

"D . . . W . . . I . . ." she muttered as she wrote the name on a sticker.

Yes, Jack thought as the movie star stuck the name tag onto the back of the woolly sheep. *Another fifty cents is mine!*

Now it was a goat's turn. Jack studied the bleating young buck for a moment before he came up with the *perfect* name: "Confucius!"

Victoria nodded and wrote that one down, too.

Jack was cleaning up! *And* he was on a roll. Naming the pig would be no problem.

Would it?

As Jack arrived at the pigpen next to the sheep and goat corral, he felt momentary panic.

Because his mind was momentarily blank!

Pig . . . pig, he said to himself. *Name for a pig. C'mon. Think!*

"Um . . . Piggy?" Jack said with a squeak.

Victoria frowned.

"I am not giving you fifty cents for Piggy," she admonished Jack. "You'll have to do better than that."

"Oh, man," Jack said, putting two fingers to his sweaty temples. "Pressure! How about . . . Cassiopeia?"

"Excellent!" Victoria cried, patting Jack on the head. She began to write the name on a sticker.

"C-a-s," she muttered, "um . . . s . . . o? Erm . . . a?"

She looked at Jack for a prompt. Jack gave her a shrug.

Victoria shrugged back and announced, "Piggy it is!"

Great, Jack thought, pumping his fist in victory. *Victoria's coming around to my way of thinking. It won't be long before she introduces me to her producer, her manager, her agent. . . . I'll be made. Hel-lo, Hollywood!*

Back at Creature Comforts, Darcy was feeling a lot

less enamored with her current task. She was totally straining her slender biceps and triceps as she dragged the heavy supplies back into the clinic. And listening to the girl behind the counter titter at her predicament *wasn't* helping matters.

Darcy was relieved when a man interrupted her. This guy was totally unlike JoJo and Snoozie. (Snoozie was the name Darcy had given to the old man napping on the bench. He hadn't moved a muscle since Darcy'd arrived!) Instead of wearing a tattered plaid shirt, the man had on a crisp, blue medical uniform. Instead of hair that was frowsy, this man's was brown and carefully combed. And instead of hauling around big bags of feed and stuff, this guy was tenderly cradling a baby pig! As a rule, Darcy was not a pig person. She was more of a poodle person. But even she had to admit—that brand-new baby pig was supercute.

"Oh, hello," the man said to Darcy. "I'm Dr. Adams, the veterinarian here at Creature Comforts. And I own it. Came up with the name for it myself. Although Lindsay and Jack had some very nice suggestions."

Dr. Adams nodded at the girl behind the counter.

So she's the vet's daughter! Darcy thought. And *Jack's sister! And lo and behold, she has a name!*

Lindsay. I was starting to wonder!

"Anyway," Dr. Adams said, regaining his train of thought. "Welcome aboard!"

Lindsay hopped out from behind the counter.

"She doesn't work here, Dad," she corrected the vet urgently. "She's a customer."

"Hmm," Dr. Adams said, stroking the baby pig's head absently. "Customers usually take products *out* the door. And we *do* need someone to replace JoJo."

Dr. Adams learned toward Darcy and whispered: "He got a job teaching philosophy at Harvard."

What?! Darcy thought.

"Or was it running the Tilt-a-Whirl at a carnival?" Dr. Adams wondered, gazing at the ceiling. Then he shrugged. "Either way, all the best to JoJo."

"Go, JoJo," Darcy shrugged.

Okay, this guy definitely has the absentminded scientist role down pat! Darcy thought. *He's pretty nice, though.*

"Are you good with money, young lady?" Dr. Adams asked her.

"I'm *very* good with money," Darcy said excitedly. "It's one of my best subjects."

"And you don't seem to mind dragging things," the vet observed. "Are you looking for a job?"

"No, Dad!" Lindsay cut in. "You don't understand—"

"No need to explain, Lindsay," Dr. Adams said,

looking pleased with himself. "I was right to begin with."

He looked into Darcy's eyes, smiled kindly, and announced, "Welcome aboard, young lady. And please, call me Kevin. Everyone does. I'd shake hands, but I've got this pig. . . ."

Darcy giggled as Kevin gazed down at the pig, as if he was wondering how it had landed in his arms in the first place.

"Lindsay," Kevin said, "I'll be in the back."

With that, the creator of Creature Comforts was gone. He left an awkward silence in his wake. Cringing, Darcy glanced at Lindsay. The girl was *fuming*.

"So," Darcy said with an apologetic grin, "I guess I work here!"

Which means I've gotten two jobs in one day, Darcy thought. *That's definitely a record for me! I wonder if Mom will give me any bonus dollars for fetching both her supplies and a gig for myself. That's pretty enterprising, if I do say so myself. I just hope I don't have to work too hard.*

"Well, you can start by getting that feed back on the shelves," Lindsay said, jabbing her thumb in the direction of Darcy's supplies.

Darcy looked at the giant bags of feed and sighed.

I just hope I don't have to work too hard, Darcy mocked herself. *Okay, how naive was that wish?*

"And don't get too comfortable," Lindsay warned her. "I'll be surprised if you last a week, Hollywood."

As Lindsay stomped into the clinic after her dad, Darcy protested, "It's *Malibu*! Why is that so hard to remember?"

Sighing, Darcy walked across the store to begin restocking her heavy supplies. As she heaved the first bag of feed onto a shelf, she consoled herself by thinking of all things she could buy with her hard-earned cash.

I'll start with an authentic pair of fur-lined Uggs. I've always wanted a pair, but southern Cali is too hot for 'em. Then I'll move onto a new skin-care system from Elizabeth Arden. This fresh air is totally making me break out. And then . . . hey, wait a minute. I just thought of something. Will I be able to afford all this merch? Maybe I should have asked Kevin what my hourly wage is gonna be. . . .

Chapter 7

Wild Wisdom . . . *When one llama is angry
at another llama, it will stick its tongue out to
express its dislike.*

After a few days working at Creature Comforts,
Darcy was feeling *much* more in-the-know. First of
all, she knew that she'd have to work approximately
52.5 hours to afford a pair of fur-lined Ugg boots.

She'd also become confident enough to do a little
decorating around the shop. Today, she was just putting the final touches on a totally cute sign.

"Stomach Worm-Go-Way," the sign said. "30%
off."

Beneath her bubbly letters, Darcy had Magic-
Markered a worm wearing a top hat, wiggling away
from a sheep that was contentedly sunning itself in a
field of pink flowers.

"There, Darce," Darcy whispered to herself as
she placed the card on the Creature Comforts counter.
"You've got this gig wired!"

Darcy was so busy smiling at her sign that she didn't hear some customers walk into the shop. When she glanced up, she gasped to find herself nose-to-nose with a big-eyed, floppy-lipped llama!

"Um, can I help you?" Darcy asked.

The two guys standing on either side of the animal answered on its behalf.

"We're here to get a toy for our llama," said the shorter guy.

"It's her birthday," said his taller brother. How did Darcy know they were brothers? The identical plaid shirts and navy baseball caps gave them away. They also wore the exact same, amiable, slightly absent-minded smiles.

And, the short guy introduced himself by saying, "I'm Brett Brennan, by the way. And this is my brother, Brandon."

"We're the Brennan brothers," Brandon confirmed.

"Hi!" Darcy said to the guys. "That's so sweet of you to buy your llama a present."

Then she turned to the animal herself.

"And how old are you today?" she asked the big (if sorta stinky) cutie.

Brandon's face went stony.

"Don't look straight at her," he ordered Darcy.

"She'll go for your eyes. She's a spitter!"

"Yeah," Brett echoed. "A spitter!"

"Heh, heh." Darcy took two big steps backward. "Uh, llama toys in back."

Brandon grabbed his pet's harness and began to lead her away.

"Let's find something you'll like, Oprah," he crooned to the llama.

Brett stayed at the counter.

"So, young lady," he said, "I need some supplies for my critters. Brandon and I take care of exotic animals."

"I noticed," Darcy said, shooting Oprah the Llama an apprehensive glance.

"Yeah, we rehabilitate 'em," Brett explained nonchalantly. "So, I need some calf manna, some psyllium fiber—the powder, not the capsules, of course—some hoof maximizer, a couple hundred pounds of scratch feed . . ."

As Brett went on and on *and on*, Darcy smiled and nodded, but inside her head, she was all, *What the* heck *is this guy talking about?!?*

※ (DARCY'S DISH) ※

Okay, my people. The guy might as well have been speaking in gibberish!

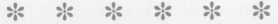

"And doobedy-bobbedy yimmity-yack," Brett went on, "gobble-de-gobble-de mumba-da-mumba-mumba, a few salt spools, *and* some equine rehydrant. Did you get all that?"

He gave Darcy a friendly, if slightly demanding, smile.

"Yeah, I got it," Darcy said wearily, "except for one part."

"What part was that?" Brett wondered.

Darcy felt megaguilty as she admitted, "The part after, 'So, young lady.'"

"I got you covered, Brett!"

Darcy jumped. That was Lindsay, coming out of the clinic in a typically practical dark, denim shirt.

"Darcy here is new," Lindsay explained as she alighted at the counter, nudging Darcy out of the way with her hip. "And, y'know, she's pretty much useless."

"Hey," Darcy protested. "I can help!"

"Fine," Lindsay challenged her. "Psyllium fiber's on that shelf."

She pointed to a very tall shelf in the corner of the shop. Darcy *never* went into this corner. That's because it was pretty much dominated by the old coot she called Snoozie. (Not out loud, of course.) Darcy had learned that this guy literally never left Creature

Comforts! With his cowboy hat pulled low over his eyes, he napped there in the mornings and rested there during lunch. He dozed away his afternoons there and just kept on sleeping into the evening for good measure. He seemed perfectly content to sleep his *life* away in Creature Comforts, and the white mouse who'd made a nest atop his hat seemed happy with the arrangement as well.

I guess I'll *have to get happy with the whole Snoozie sitch, too,* Darcy thought nervously.

Scratch that. As soon as she reached for the psyllium fiber—which, of course, was on the highest shelf Lindsay could have found—Darcy realized that Snoozie was *so* in her way.

"Excuse me? Hello?" she said to the snoring old man.

She nudged him gently on the shoulder. He didn't stir a muscle.

"Boy, I hope you're not dead," she whispered.

She sighed. She was just going to have reach around Snoozie to get to the psyllium powder. She stood on the tiptoes of her high-heeled shoes and stretched for the bottle of mysterious animal stuff. She was reaching . . . reaching . . .

"Darcy!"

"Ah!" Darcy squeaked. She jumped away from the shelf and spun around to see Jack Adams, standing in the middle of Creature Comforts. With a goat. On a leash.

Okay, she asked herself. *Will the weirdness of this place never cease?*

Completely ignoring her annoyed expression, Jack exclaimed, "Excellent. Watch this!"

"I'm a little busy right now, Jack," Darcy huffed.

"You just have to watch," Jack insisted. "I've taught her to tap-dance. You'll tell your mom about it, she'll tell her showbiz friends, and I'll be on a plane to Hollywood!"

Darcy rolled her eyes. But she supposed even a tap-dancing goat was more interesting than psyllium fiber, so she nodded at Jack.

Jack turned to the goat.

"And . . . go!" he yelled, pointing at the goat and tapping his own foot.

The goat stood there. No tapping. Not even a little hip waggle.

Jack shook his head and tried again.

"And . . . go!" he urged.

The goat . . . didn't.

"And . . . go!" Jack cried desperately, waving his hands at his pet.

The goat was so still, Darcy wondered if he was made of stone. A goat statue.

"And . . . *go!*" Jack screeched.

No go.

Finally, the squirt gave up.

"We'll keep working on it," he assured Darcy. Darcy grimaced as Jack led the nondancing goat out of Creature Comforts.

"What are you embarrassing me for?" he whispered to the critter.

Chapter 8

Wild Wisdom . . . *Pythons have two lungs (most snakes have only one) and the remnants of hind legs and pelvic bones.*

After Jack and his stubborn goat had left Creature Comforts, Darcy sighed and shook her head.

As if I didn't have enough strikes against me here, she complained silently, *nobody will let me do the work that Lindsay thinks I can't do.*

Scowling with determination, Darcy went back to groping for the psyllium fiber. The distant bottle was *almost* in her grasp when—

"Skittles needs her shots!"

"Eek!" Darcy cried. She whirled around to see who had interrupted her psyllium quest *this* time. It was a girl with thick red braids and a pug dog in her arms.

Before Darcy had a chance to say a word, Lindsay popped out of the clinic, holding a broom.

"Hey, Hollywood," she said, eyeing the dusty floor under Snoozie's feet. She stalked across the shop and handed Darcy the broom. "You clean up. I'll take Skittles here back for her shots."

Lindsay scooped the pup out of the girl's arms and darted back to the clinic. Darcy began a sulky floor sweep, but soon her broom was blocked by a pair of scuffed Skechers. She looked up. The red-haired girl was standing right in front of her, transfixed. Shocked, even. It took the girl a full minute before she could make a single sound.

But once she got her first word out, many, *many* tumbled after it.

"Omigosh!" the girl gushed. "I've seen you on TV. On the Celebrity Mother/Daughter Fashion channel? I can't believe you really moved here!"

She stared at Darcy some more, her mouth open.

"Um . . . hi," Darcy said. "Darcy Fields."

"Oh!" the girl burst out. "Kathi Giraldi. I can't believe I'm meeting somebody who's been to a real movie premiere. Are they great?!"

"Yeah!" Darcy said. Not only was this Kathi girl being nice to her (unlike a certain Lindsay Adams) she seemed to . . . *worship* her. Cool!

"I mean," Darcy qualified her answer, "if you consider wearing gorgeous clothes and hanging out with movie stars and staying up all night dancing great."

"I do! I do!" Kathi cried. "The closest thing here was when my dad's car dealership—my dad owns a car dealership—had a Presidents' Day Sale-a-bration where they had free popcorn and a professional Cher impersonator. He sounded *just* like her. Anyway, it's great to meet you."

Darcy was just starting to enjoy basking in Kathi's gushy outreach when she heard Kevin's voice behind her.

"Darcy? Could you give me a hand? Oh, hi, Kathi."

While Kathi peeked over Darcy's shoulder to wave to the vet, Darcy said, "Nice to meet you, Kathi. I'm sure I'll see you around."

Then she turned around, fully intending to help her employer with whatever he needed, until—

"Yagggggh!" Darcy screamed.

She hadn't considered that Kevin might have needed help with a snake! A very *large* snake. A python, in fact! It was draped around Kevin's neck, looking depressed.

"Shhh," Kevin admonished Darcy. "Don't scare her."

"Don't scare her?" Darcy blurted. "Don't scare *me*!"

"Lily's anorexic," the vet explained. "She's starving

54

herself. So, she needs enteric fluids. You hold her
coils while I give her a shot."

DARCY'S DISH

Great. I just got this job, and I already have to
wrestle a snake that thinks it's a supermodel!

Darcy looked at Kevin in horror.

"Do you mean, hold the snake's coils as in . . .
touch it?"

"Unless," Kevin said, looking excited, "you'd
rather force-feed her a dead mouse."

Darcy cringed and shook her head hard. Then she
took a reluctant step toward the python. She extended
a few tentative fingertips toward her.

Ugh! She shrieked inside. *No way can I do this!*

She drew her hands back, recoiling from Lily's
shiny coils.

On the other hand, if I don't do this, she warned
herself, *I'll totally lose this job.*

Biting her lip, Darcy tried to touch the snake
again. She was within seconds—okay, maybe minutes—of making contact with Lily's cold, scaly skin
when she felt that familiar nudge on her arm.

"I'm done with the dog," Lindsay said, moving

Darcy aside. "I'll do this."

"Oh," Darcy said. She didn't know whether to be indignant at being ousted, or relieved. She chose relieved.

"Okay," she breathed. "So, what should I do?"

"Take Skittles back to her owner," Lindsay said, plunking the pug into Darcy's arms. "Then think about trying to find a job you can actually do."

Darcy walked slowly across the shop, feeling totally stung. Even cuddling Kathi's little pug didn't help.

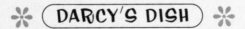

That's right, my people. Those were Lindsay's exact words: "a job you can actually do." I mean, okay, so I couldn't deal with a snake. And, yeah, I didn't understand what any of the customers were saying. And I don't know what any of our products are, or what they do. But does that mean I'm unqualified?

Darcy hadn't felt this bad since . . . well, since her mother had announced that they were moving to Bailey! Lindsay had made it very clear—a teenage girl from Malibu and the country folk of Bailey just *didn't* mix!

Darcy's funk continued after she got off work.

Dragging herself down Main Street, she got no comfort at all from the dowdy clothes shops, deep-fried cafés, and multiple seed-and-feed stores lining the sidewalks.

I just don't belong *here*, she thought glumly. *Nothing fits, nothing makes sense—wait a minute!*

Darcy had just spotted a shop window that *did* make sense to her, even if the word decaled on the glass was in a foreign language: "Gelato!"

Gelato's the best thing to come out of Italy since Gucci! Darcy thought, her steps quickening.

❋ (DARCY'S DISH) ❋

Luckily, in these dark moments, I can always cheer myself up with some calories.

Darcy had almost reach the gelato shop. She could practically taste the superrich, Italian ice cream already.

But then, the truck parked in front of the store pulled away, and Darcy skidded to a halt. The truck had been hiding half of the shop's sign.

That doesn't say gelato, Darcy wailed in her head. *It says Gelatovich Manure Supply. So not the same thing!*

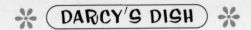 DARCY'S DISH

Not this time. My dreams of ice-cream therapy fell flat.

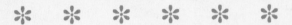

For a moment, Darcy considered getting a consolation cone at Bailey's *actual* ice-cream store, the Dairee King, but after she'd envisioned herself eating hazelnut mocha gelato, soft-serve vanilla just wasn't going to cut it.

Hanging her head, she simply wandered home.

Chapter 9

And when she got home, was anybody waiting for her in the kitchen, anxious to greet her with an after-work snack or even a hello?

Uh, no.

Darcy's house was empty, and there was nobody in the animal pens except animals with name tags clinging to their fur. Clearly, Jack had finished all his naming (not to mention goat dance lessons) and moved onto something else. And, since Darcy couldn't hear any crashes, bangs, or crackling of flames in the air, it appeared Eli was AWOL as well.

"Mom?" Darcy called out. She headed to the barn. "Where is everybody?"

As it turned out, everybody was in the barn. Victoria was in the horse stall. Eli was lounging around on some hay bales. And Kevin was—

Wait a minute, Darcy thought. *Kevin? What's he doing here?*

Victoria gazed at Darcy. She looked as serious as a movie star in a bright orange head scarf and a baby pink duster can look.

"Hi, Sweetie," Victoria said. "Gus doesn't seem to be feeling well. It would appear he ate some pot-pourri."

Darcy's hand flew to her mouth.

"Omigosh," she cried. "I sprinkled it around while I was mucking out the stall."

Eli gaped, Kevin gasped, and Victoria shook her head sorrowfully.

"I mean," Darcy added defensively, "this place doesn't exactly smell like fresh-baked cookies."

"Well, Gus is having an allergic reaction," Kevin said. "You have to be careful what you leave in animals' reach. I once left a bottle of shampoo where a badger could get it. He burped soap bubbles for a week!"

"Will Gus be okay?" Darcy said with a squeak. She felt totally guilty. Sure, she and Gus hadn't gotten off on the best foot. Or hoof. Or whatever. But still, Darcy never meant to hurt the big guy. Over the past few days, she'd even come to like the horse. His soft white nose and velvety brown ears were softer than the most expensive suede jacket. And once he was *far* away from

his mucky stall, he didn't smell half bad for a barnyard
animal.

"I've given Gus an antihistamine shot," Kevin
reported. "That should reduce the edema. But he has
to be monitored for the next twelve hours to make sure
that the swelling in his throat doesn't come back."

"What if it does?" Victoria said, putting a hand to
her own throat.

"He could suffocate," Kevin said.

Darcy gasped.

How could I have done this? she thought in anguish.

"Now, I've got to drive over to Kimbrow County,"
Kevin said, stashing some supplies in his vet's bag.
"They've got a herd of sick sheep. So someone's going
to have to stay with Gus all night."

Darcy bit her lip. She so wanted to be there for
Gus. But was she up to the job? Lindsay sure wouldn't
think so.

But Lindsay's not here, Darcy thought. *And Kevin's
leaving, too. Which basically means, I'm all Gus has. I
owe it to him. . . .*

Darcy raised her hand.

"I'll do it," she said softly. "I'll stay with Gus."

Darcy was aware of her mother's proud look,
but she didn't have time to bask in it. She had to pay

attention to Kevin's instructions.

"Excellent," Kevin said. "Keep him on his feet. You'll have to monitor his breathing. If it gets labored, give him another shot, like I've shown you at the clinic. I've prepared a few needles. Now where are they?"

As Kevin, Darcy, and Victoria looked around the barn, Eli, still sitting on his hay bale, suddenly got a very strange look on his face.

"Um," he asked Kevin, "did you by any chance set those needles on a hay bale?"

"I did," Kevin remembered.

"Oh, man," Eli said, getting to his feet. A long syringe was sticking out of the seat of his pants!

"Am I gonna die?" Eli squeaked.

Kevin laughed and walked across the barn to pull the needle out of Eli's backside.

"Don't worry," Kevin assured him. "It won't damage you. You'll just be in excruciating pain for the next twenty-four hours."

"Eep!" Eli gasped.

"Come on," Kevin said, throwing an arm around Eli's shoulders. "I'll drop you off at home."

Darcy walked over to say good-bye. Kevin handed her a stethoscope.

"Gus is counting on you," he said, looking straight

into Darcy's blue eyes.

I know, Darcy thought with a gulp. *I just hope Gus knows what he's doing, counting on a girl who wouldn't know psyllium fiber from salt spools. The same goes for Kevin and my mom. What if I let them down?!*

Kevin left the barn, with Eli hobbling alongside him. "Ow," Eli groaned with every step. "Ow. Ow. Ow."

Darcy took a deep breath and started for the horse stall. It was going to be a *long* night.

And it started out seriously tense. Darcy and her mother paced back and forth in front of Gus's stall. They must have crisscrossed back and forth five hundred times! Every time they finished a lap, one of them would peek in on the ailing horse, listening for raspy breathing, snorts of discomfort, hoof-stomps of pain . . . anything and everything.

It was torture! Especially, when Gus started doing some pretty weird things. For one, he exhaled so hard, his rubbery horse lips flapped around! The first time she saw him do this, Darcy ran to his side, the stethoscope in one hand and a syringe full of medicine in the other.

But Darcy's mom stopped her from giving Gus the shot. Victoria had made a Western or two during her Hollywood days, so she was able to assure Darcy about that flappy-lip thing. It was apparently just something horses did.

Who knew? Darcy thought.

The cool thing was, after about an hour of keen observation, Darcy *did* know. She also picked up a few other horsey facts. She learned that horses swung their tails around to swat at flies and that they loved it when you stroked their velvety noses.

After a few hours of watching and learning, Darcy started to feel like she actually had some horse sense. She figured out that stroking Gus's throat made him more comfortable and whispering in his ear eased his anxiety.

But did it make Darcy and Victoria less nervous? Not even! The horse-sitters had hours to go before they could sleep.

Chapter 10

Wild Wisdom . . . *There are more chickens in the world than any other domesticated bird—more than one chicken for every human.*

It was now 10:00 PM. Darcy was just starting to feel tired.

Unfortunately, Gus was just starting to act really sick! His breathing, which had been loud and raspy all evening, became labored and wheezy. Darcy and her mother rushed to his side. After Victoria tried to listen to Gus's chest—and placed the stethoscope in the wrong spot completely—Darcy put on the medical device and listened herself.

Close up, Gus's breathing didn't sound as scary as she'd thought. Darcy decided, nervously, that he wasn't in enough trouble to warrant another shot.

Yet.

So she and her mom returned to their nervous pacing. But when their feet started throbbing from all that walking, Victoria finally suggested a game of checkers to pass the time between Gus checks. Darcy played along, but she was so focused on the horse that before she knew it, she'd kinged half of Victoria's red checkers. Soon after, her mom won the game, and Darcy didn't even care.

All she wanted was for Gus to get better.

That desire gave Darcy the strength to keep up the horse watch as the moon rose higher over the barn. It made her pinch herself to stay awake, even after her mother had dozed off on top of a couple hay bales. Darcy covered Victoria with a grassy-smelling horse blanket and returned to Gus's side, patting him and whispering to him.

Around 2:00 AM, Gus really started to wheeze. Darcy listened to the horse's heaving chest for about the hundredth time. But this time, her heart sank as she listened.

"Omigosh, boy," she whispered, biting her lip. "You sound awful."

Darcy felt a wave of panic wash over her, but she quickly tamped it down. Gus needed her.

And suddenly, Darcy felt certain she *was* up to the task.

"It's okay," she said to Gus as she rubbed the

wooziness out of her eyes. "We're gonna make
you better."

She hurried to her mom's makeshift bed and shook
Victoria's shoulder gently.

"Mom," she whispered. "We've got to give Gus
another shot."

Snooorrrre.

Darcy sighed. When Victoria Fields started snoring,
she was definitely out for the night. Shooting all those
movies in exotic locations had made her immune to
both jet lag and insomnia. She could sleep through a
train wreck.

Or an equine crisis, Darcy thought, her brow fur-
rowed. Squaring her shoulders, she went and picked
up one of the horse shots. Holding it behind her back
(so Gus wouldn't get scared), she stepped into the
horse's stall and stroked his neck.

"Okay, it's just you and me, Gus," she said quietly.
"But don't worry—I got you into this, and I won't let
you down."

Darcy pulled the syringe out and felt for the pre-
cise spot above Gus's shoulder where Kevin had
taught her to give the injection. Gus seemed fine with
the whole shot thing, but with one look at the superlong needle, *Darcy* started to feel freaked. Before she

could stick the needle into the horse's muscle, she asked him, "What'd you have to eat my potpourri for anyway?"

Gus did his lip-flappy thing and shook his head a bit.

"I know, I know," Darcy shrugged. "Who can resist cinnamon-mulberry?"

Holding the needle an inch away from Gus's warm, brown shoulder, she shook her head.

"I'm so sorry this happened to you," she said. She gave Gus one more pat before taking a deep breath and muttering, "Okay, here goes. . . ."

As gently as she could, Darcy plunged the needle through Gus's soft coat, then injected the medicine. Gus barely flinched.

What a brave horse, Darcy thought.

To Gus, she said, "Boy, I hope this works!"

It did work! After about an hour of fretful watching, Darcy saw a change in Gus's breathing. But with several hours left in the horse's twelve-hour danger zone, she knew she couldn't let down her guard. She paced his stall some more. And when she ran out of energy for pacing, she leaned against Gus's solid flank.

She rubbed her eyes and tapped herself on her cheeks, mumbling, "Stay awake . . . stay awake."

She played word games in her head and counted the boards in the barn ceiling. She listened to Gus's chest every fifteen minutes and kept up a running monologue with the horse about her glam life back home.

At the moment, that life seemed so far away, it was hard to imagine. And if Darcy hadn't been so tired, she might have noticed that this didn't seem like such a bad thing. Maybe she was even starting to get used to dowdy old Bailey.

Or maybe that was just the sleep deprivation talking. Either way, when the sun finally began to rise, Darcy was stunned to realize that she'd done it. She'd actually done it! She hadn't bailed on Gus even once, and now the night was almost over!

Chapter 11

Wild Wisdom . . . *Globally, more people drink goat's milk than cow's milk.*

By the time the Fields' rooster crowed, others were starting to stir as well. Victoria awoke with a big, loud yawn and a yoga-honed stretch. And Lindsay appeared in the barn door, wearing a kelly green polo shirt and a stethoscope around her neck. Darcy was leaning on a hay bale by then, too tired to even waggle her fingers at the visitor or rasp out a hello.

It was only when Lindsay stepped up to Gus and began examining him with her stethoscope that Darcy found the fuel to jump to her feet.

"Lindsay," she cried. "Don't worry, I'm awake."

Completely out of my head from lack of sleep, but awake, she qualified silently. *Awake enough to know that Lindsay's checking up on me. I wonder what she'll say.*

Lindsay straightened up and gave Gus a pat. He

whinnied in return, and it wasn't a wheezy whinny. It was strong and hardly raspy at all!

"It's okay, Darcy," Lindsay said. "He looks fine."

Darcy nodded, but she didn't really hear what Lindsay was saying. She was too fuzzy from exhaustion.

"I gave him a shot," Darcy slurred. "Two."

Wait, that doesn't sound right.

"Not two shots," Darcy corrected herself carefully. "One shot, at two in the morning."

"Good," Lindsay said matter-of-factly. "His breathing is normal. It seems to have worked."

"Checked him every hour," Darcy went on, staggering a bit on her feet. "Didn't sleep."

She staggered a bit more.

"Feel dizzy," she murmured. Then she looked around the barn. Cute little polka dots were buzzing around her head. Was that normal?

"See spots!" she blurted. She reached out and tried to grab one of the pretty little spots—a pink one, her favorite color. Alas, the moment she tried to catch it, the thingy evaporated.

"You should probably go in the house and get some sleep," Lindsay said with a half smile.

Darcy's eyes went wide. (And boy were they dry and scratchy, too.)

"I can't sleep," she insisted. "I have to be at work soon!"

"No," Lindsay insisted. "You don't. We're going to get along without you."

What? Darcy balked. *So, just as Lindsay predicted, I've been fired? Canned? Pink-slipped?! And just as I was getting a handle on my new gig. Staying up with Gus all night might have saved his life, but it didn't save me my job. Man, the work world is harsh!*

Darcy might have said all this to Lindsay, but her tongue suddenly felt as fuzzy and immobile as a mossy rock. All she could muster was a pathetic, "Oh . . ."

"Wait," Lindsay said. "I mean *today!* We can get along without you *today.*"

Wait a minute, Darcy wondered blearily. *Does this mean I'm not fired?*

As if she'd heard Darcy's thoughts, Lindsay explained, "You've been up all night taking care of a patient. You have to get some rest."

Darcy shot Gus a look. She was incredulous and elated, and she totally wanted to share the moment with her now-healthy horse.

Gus looked thoroughly nonplussed, but to Darcy, this was a big, big deal. She'd actually been successful at giving a creature comfort! And she wasn't going to be fired. Lindsay was even looking impressed with her!

"So . . . I can do this job?" Darcy asked her.

Lindsay looked Darcy up and down, just as she had on the day they'd first met. Darcy was wearing a shirred yellow top, accented with a pretty, pink ruffle; boot-cut, perfectly distressed jeans; and a frothy scarf for a belt. For a moment, Darcy felt self-conscious.

I know just what Lindsay's thinking, she realized. *This outfit doesn't exactly scream, "farm girl"!*

But another glance at the contented Gus made Darcy revise her self-criticism.

On the other hand, she told herself, *how many other farm girls could stay up all night with their sick horses and look stylish at the same time? What's wrong with having both horse sense and fashion sense? I say, nothing!*

And maybe Lindsay agreed! Because her face suddenly softened, and a smile tugged at her lips.

"You can do this job," she assured Darcy. "See you tomorrow, Hollywood."

She turned to head out of the barn, but stopped herself, glancing back at Darcy over her shoulder.

"I mean," she corrected herself, "see you tomorrow, *Malibu.*"

Darcy was sleep-deprived and hungry. Bits of hay were stuck to her cute outfit, and she was scratching away at several horsefly bites. After pacing the barn all night in her high heels, her feet were killing her. But at that moment, she couldn't have been happier.

Forgetting her sore tootsies, Darcy practically skipped out of the barn. But not before pausing to give Gus a grateful pat and a kiss on his velvety nose.

She couldn't wait get to her computer to update Darcy's Dish. Apparently she'd been wrong— exciting things could happen in Bailey, from all-night horse dramas to . . . tap-dancing goats?!

That's right. When Darcy emerged from the barn, she came upon Jack Adams, future Hollywood huckster, leading his pet goat in a snazzy little two-step.

"Hey, everybody, look!" Jack called out as the goat's hooves tapped delicately in the dirt. "He's doing it!"

Darcy laughed as her mother—still bleary after her snooze on the hay bale—stumbled out of the barn behind her.

While her mother began heaping sleepy praise onto Jack, Darcy headed for the house, where her computer awaited.

❋ (DARCY'S DISH) ❋

So that's what happened, folks. One minute I was on the red carpet with my mom, the next, I was living in Bailey and even had a job. Looks like I'm here to stay—I'm going to be living in a place I don't understand, and doing all kinds of gross stuff with weird animals who scare the pants off me. And here's the strangest part! I can't wait!

❋ ❋ ❋ ❋ ❋ ❋

Chapter 12

Wild Wisdom . . . *The ponds created by the dams are the beaver's first defense against predators.*

Darcy knew she wouldn't have to wait long for more gross, weird, and scary animal encounters. But she didn't expect to experience all *three* of those things—gross, weird, and scary, that was—in one afternoon!

It all started after another arduous day at Creature Comforts. As Darcy walked home from work, she indulged in a little multitasking, blogging from her PDA as she strolled. (One perk of not yet having her driver's license—it was totally safe to e-communicate during her commute!)

❋ **DARCY'S DISH** ❋

Hey, people! I'm coming at you wireless. It was another bizarre day in Bailey. Remember the Brennan brothers? The ones who rehabilitate exotic animals? Check out this picture. . . .

❋   ❋   ❋   ❋   ❋   ❋

Darcy used her PDA pointer to drag a JPEG onto her website. In the photo, Brett and Brandon Brennan were cradling a fat beaver between them. She couldn't have said who was grinning harder—the plaid-shirted men or the buck-toothed beaver.

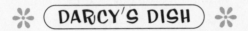

DARCY'S DISH

So, they brought their beaver into Creature Comforts, 'cause it had a sore on its tail. And I had to hold it while Kevin put ointment on it.

As Darcy turned onto the front walk of her cozy farmhouse, she paused in her scribbling to glare at her hands.

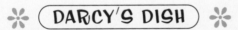

DARCY'S DISH

That beav totally chewed up my fingernails, after I'd spent all morning stenciling flowers on them! Roses! Like they had at Whitney Steinberg's bat mitzvah.

Darcy sighed at the memory of Whitney's magnificent bat mitzvah party. At the beauty-themed soiree, she'd gotten hot-pink highlights in her hair and a spray-on tan in addition to those too-cute-to-live nail stencils.

Those were the days, Darcy sighed as she went back to her blog.

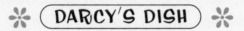

DARCY'S DISH

Beavers aren't supposed to chew fingernails. How're you going to build a dam out of fingernails?

Darcy gave her PDA pen a rest to open the kitchen door and cruise inside.

"Hi, Mom," she said. Victoria was hunched behind her newspaper at the kitchen table. Apparently, she was so immersed, she didn't even hear Darcy come in, much less say hello.

Darcy shrugged and returned to Darcy's Dish.

DARCY'S DISH

So anyway, I obviously had to get a fresh mani. In Malibu, of course, that's no biggie. But guess where you have to go in Bailey to get your nails done? Try the hardware store! Yup, they've got all the nails you want—if you want to hang a picture or hammer a couple boards together! It's tragic, I know, but that's life on a ranch. If it gets any weirder, I'll let you know.

Darcy rolled her eyes and grinned before upload-
ing her blog entry onto her website. Then she
plopped down at the kitchen table across from
Victoria, who was still mesmerized by her newspaper.

"So, what's for dinner, Mom?" she asked.

Even as the words left her mouth, Darcy shook her
head in disbelief. In addition to adjusting to Bailey,
she was still getting used to her movie-star mom suddenly being so down-home. Used to be, Victoria read
the newspaper simply to keep tabs on the news about
herself and her celebrated acting career. She didn't
cook dinner, she ordered dinner. And when she did, it
was usually filet mignon or lobster. During the rare
moments she had to sit around the house, Victoria
was usually outfitted in something silky and flowy,
with marabou trim and full hair and makeup. She
wasn't wearing her current outfit: a pair of denim
overalls, big square glasses, and . . . big, yellow teeth,
and a bod covered with dark brown hair?!

"Eeeeeee!" screeched the figure behind the newspaper, who Darcy now realized, of course, was *not* her
mother at all but a chimpanzee!

Darcy gaped at the gangly, and frankly angry-
looking, animal. A full minute went by before she
remembered to breathe. Then, very slowly and

carefully, so as not to startle the ape sitting across the dinner table, she picked up her PDA again.

Okay, it just got weirder. . .

Chapter 13

Wild Wisdom . . . *Chimpanzees are called our closest living relative because they share all but 1.4 percent of our DNA.*

No sooner had Darcy posted this last morsel of information than the chimp *went nuts*! He opened his big mouth, screeched so loud that Darcy could smell his breath from six feet away, and waved his long, sinewy arms at her.

"Eeeeeek!" Darcy shrieked, jumping out of her chair and dashing from the room. She cowered in the hallway outside the kitchen with her fingers crossed, desperately hoping the chimp would get up and leave.

When, after a few minutes, Darcy heard no pitter-patter of chimpy feet, she peeked around the doorjamb. The chimp was still sitting at the table, but instead of reading his newspaper, he was now glaring at Darcy!

Darcy bit her lip.

Okay, she told herself, *clearly this guy isn't going anywhere. I guess my only choice is to try to make friends with him.*

She tiptoed back into the kitchen, fixed the chimp with a wobbly smile, and said with a squeak, "Are you filling in for Eli? You probably make better pancakes than he does!"

The chimp was clearly not taken in by Darcy's compliment. In fact, he pooched out his lips and blew a big razzberry at her!

"Though Eli is more polite," Darcy admonished the ape with a cold stare.

Before he had a chance to make another noisy retort, Darcy's mother swished into the kitchen in a cloud of perfume. She was wearing a smart red blouse and had her curls pinned into an elaborate updo on top of her head.

"Hi, Sweetie," she said to Darcy absently as she made a beeline for the fridge. She hummed to herself as she pulled out a pitcher of iced tea, loaded with mint leaves and lemon slices.

Like they say, Darcy thought with an indulgent smile, *you can take the girl out of Hollywood, but you can't take the Hollywood out of the girl. Speaking of which, let's see how long it takes Mom to: A) spot the wild beast in the middle of our kitchen, and B) totally freak!*

Victoria took a big swallow of iced tea and sat at the kitchen table. She chose a chair only *two feet away* from the chimpanzee, who'd gone back to reading the newspaper.

Victoria rearranged some fruit in the big bowl on the kitchen island and took another sip. Then she gave Darcy a nice, momlike smile and said, "How was work?"

What?! How was work? Darcy screamed inside. *Try, "How do you feel about a fuzzy ape taking up residence in our kitchen?!"*

But Darcy held her tongue. She really wanted to know: Was her mother totally oblivious? Or totally playing with Darcy's head?!

So Darcy shrugged her shoulders and reported, "Work was good. Flea-dipped a prairie dog."

"Oh," Victoria said before taking another slurp of iced tea. "Interesting."

Darcy stared at her mom. She stared at her with hard and squinty eyes. Surely Victoria must have felt the heat of Darcy's scrutiny, but she refused to bite. She simply slurped some more and gazed contentedly out the kitchen window.

Finally, Darcy gave up the game and sputtered, "I'm not going to do it, Mom. I'm not going to be the one to ask what a chimp is doing in our kitchen!"

"I should think it's obvious," Victoria said, motioning to the chimp's newspaper. "He's reading the comics!"

As Darcy rolled her eyes, the kitchen door opened and the Brennan brothers marched in. As usual, they were dressed alike and standing elbow to elbow.

"Heya, Darce," Brett said. "What's going on?"

"Not much," Darcy said drily. "Chimpanzee's reading *The Wizard of Id*."

"Oooh!" both brothers exclaimed together. "Lemme see!"

They clambered to the table and stood behind the chimp, peering at the funnies over his shoulders.

Darcy huffed and threw up her hands.

Okay, did I wake up in the Twilight Zone *this morning?* she wondered. *Or is somebody going to explain to me what's going on here?*

Finally, Victoria seemed to get a whiff of Darcy's frustration.

"The Brennan brothers," she explained, "have adopted Baron von Chimpie."

"Baron?" Darcy said.

This dude's a royal?! she thought. *Well, I guess I*

_can see that. Those sticky-outtie ears of his do kind of
remind me of Prince Charles. Although, speaking of
princes . . ._

"See, I would have called him Prince Hairy,"
Darcy quipped out loud.

Her mother looked at her blankly.

"Hairy?" Darcy added with a goofy grin. "Y'know,
because he's covered with hair?"

Victoria didn't laugh. She didn't even crack
a smile.

I guess I'm not exactly ready for the borscht belt,
Darcy thought. She felt a bit deflated until the
Brennan brothers burst out laughing, giving each
other shoulder slaps and elbow nudges and everything.

"Well," Darcy said to her mother smugly, "_they_
thought I was funny."

"Man," Brett said, pointing at the newspaper,
"that Garfield cracks me up."

Okay, so they didn't think I was funny, Darcy
thought with a wince. _Let's just move along, shall we?_

Victoria gestured gracefully at their furry house-
guest and said, "Baron von Chimpie used to be a
performing chimp. His trainer quit the business, so
he needed a new home."

Darcy sniffed the air, then wrinkled her nose.

"Well, as long as his new home has a bathtub," she pointed out, "I guess he'll be fine."

"Do you want to know the really weird thing?" Victoria said, leaning on her elbows to get into gossip mode.

"Wait," Darcy blurted. "It gets *weirder*?"

"I actually worked with the Baron once," her mother said. "On *Death Knocks at Midnight*. He was a professional and a gentleman."

While Victoria shot the Baron an affectionate glance, Darcy said, "So, how come he's in our kitchen instead of making the sequel or something?"

"He doesn't do sequels," Brett explained bluntly.

"Enough about him," Brandon chimed in. "*We're* going to Pamplona to run with the bulls!"

"*Olé!*" Brett whooped, running briskly in place.

And the brothers are telling me this, why? Darcy wondered.

"So, we'll be babysitting the Baron for a few days while Brett and Brandon are out of town," Victoria said with a smile.

"Okay," Darcy said breezily. "Well, that's cool, I guess. Hey, lemme see something."

Feeling a bit giddy from the bizarreness of this whole scenario, Darcy picked up a section of the

Baron's newspaper and rifled through it.

"Here we go," she said loopily. "Sagittarius. 'You will babysit a chimpanzee.'"

She looked around at the grown-ups and shrugged.

"Well, that's so vague, it could mean anything!"

Darcy waited smugly for Brett, Brandon, and her mom to burst out laughing.

Nothing!

C'mon people? Darcy thought. *A titter? A tiny chuckle? Something?!*

Wasn't happening. The others were completely straight-faced!

Okay, folks, Darcy thought irritably. *If we're going to get through this, we all have to keep our senses of humor! Laugh with me here. Please?*

"*Eee! Eee! Eee!*"

It was the Baron! He was grinning widely and making screechy, laughing sounds!

"Well, *he* thought it was funny," she defended herself to the humans.

"Nah," Brett said, crossing his arms over his barrel chest. "That's means he's feeling gassy."

Sure enough, the Baron made a loud sound that was *much* ruder than a razzberry. Smellier, too.

Ew! Darcy thought, pinching her nose. *After this place, Creature Comforts is going to seem like a breath of fresh air.*

Chapter 14

Wild Wisdom . . . *Some fish don't mind being out of water—flying fish make long leaps out of the water, especially when they are chased by hungry predators.*

The next day at Darcy's vet job, the ambiance was *definitely* less stinky.

Glamorous, on the other hand, it wasn't. In fact, as Darcy and Lindsay stocked shelves with various dewormers, flea and tick zappers, udder salves, and hoof creams, the place was excruciatingly quiet. A big, fat cat was curled up on the Creature Comforts's counter, snoring softly. Snoozie was in his usual spot on the bench near the window, his hat pulled low, his breathing deep and even. Even his pet mouse was asleep, curled cutely in the hollow of Snoozie's hat.

Jack wasn't asleep, but he was definitely bored— bored enough to be building a log cabin out of jumbo dog cookies.

The only animated person in the joint was Kathi.

But, let's face it, Kathi was always *animated*.

"So," she was burbling. "My dad says if he can get sales up at his dealership by, like, thirty percent, he can afford to take us to Paris!"

"Paris is the best!" Darcy cooed as she heaved a heavy sack of . . . *something* onto a shelf. "The fashions. The French food. You will *so* love Paris."

Darcy was just starting to swoon over memories of Chanel and Comme des Garçons, of coffee and fresh croissants at sidewalk cafés, when Kathi cut in.

"Actually," she corrected Darcy cheerfully, "it's Paris, Texas. My dad's cousin Birdy lives there. Near a water park. *And* a snake farm!"

"Well . . ." Darcy struggled to look enthused. "That sounds awesome, too."

It sounded *so* awesome that even Lindsay was distracted from her work. She joined the girls to hear the rest of Kathi's tale.

"So, anyway," Kathi said, tossing a red pigtail over one shoulder, "Dad's giving out these as a promotion."

She handed Darcy and Lindsay each a . . . mousetrap. Lindsay peered at the contraption, which had a caption.

" 'Don't get caught without a Giraldi car or

truck,' " she read in her usual matter-of-fact mono-
tone. She handed Kathi back the trap.

"That's nice," she said. "Nothing like a dead
rodent to get you in a mood to buy."

"I know," Kathi said, rolling her eyes. "Mouse-
traps are kind of gross. I told him he should give
out little pink pooper-scoopers."

Oh man, Darcy thought, sighing. *Kathi means
well, but* pooper-scoopers? *That would* not *fly on
Rodeo Drive.*

Suddenly, Darcy gasped. She had the perfect
idea—something that *would* play in L.A. . . . and
beyond!

"You could make a commercial," Darcy suggested
to Kathi. "That's what we'd do in Hollywood."

Darcy heard a clatter—the clatter of a dog-biscuit
log cabin falling apart. Clearly her suggestion had
startled Jack. Over the remains of his dog-biscuit
architecture, he was staring at Darcy, his eyes wide
and hungry.

"Hollywood?" he squeaked.

Darcy rolled her eyes and turned her attention
back to Kathi.

"A really good commercial," she said with a knowing nod. "That's the way to reach people."

"Reach people?" Lindsay scoffed. "Her dad could go door to door for one afternoon and reach everybody in town. And probably get some free pie!"

"No! A commercial would be great!" Jack said with starry eyes. "You could start with a big battle in space and a planet explodes! Then a spaceship lands on Earth and some aliens get out—and they're looking for a great deal on an extended cab 4x4 with tinted windows!"

Lindsay stared at Jack for a moment, then turned to Darcy with a bored expression.

"Just ignore my brother," she coached her. "I do."

Meanwhile, Kathi was looking dubious.

"Jack," she said, "that sounds kind of expensive to make."

"I've got a better idea!" Jack countered without a blink. He pointed a chubby finger at Darcy. "Get Darcy's mom. She's a famous movie star."

He clapped his hands together.

"Bang! Genius!" he commended himself.

Wistfully, Darcy flashed back to her old life of red carpets and Rodeo Drive shopping sprees. Then she shook her head at Jack.

"It's a good idea," she said, "but I've asked my

mom to go back to acting a million times. She wouldn't do it. She gave up being a movie star to move here so I could 'grow up normal.'"

She stopped herself and tilted her head, listening to the phrase jangle in her ears.

"Nope, no matter how many times I say that, it just doesn't make sense."

As she sighed, Jack clenched his fists.

"She's got to do it!" he cried. "And once she does, she'll get all excited about acting again, and she'll want to be a movie star again, and I'll be part of her posse, and then I'll be riding that sweet, Hollywood gravy train."

While Jack gasped for air after that greedy, run-on sentence, Darcy turned to Lindsay.

"You know that 'ignore him' idea, Lindsay?" she asked. "Bang! Genius!"

Turned out, Kathi had been way ahead of Darcy on the whole ignoring-Jack front. While he'd been prattling on about Hollywood, *she'd* been hatching an idea of her own. And now, with her green eyes glittering, she sprung it on Darcy.

"Well, if your mom won't do the commercial, Darcy," she said, "would you?"

Darcy's mouth dropped open. Suddenly, she felt

her own eyes glittering, too! Who cared if she was simply standing in dowdy old Creature Comforts? In her mind, she was basking in the sparkle of stardom. She could practically feel the heat of the movie camera, see the flash of paparazzi flashbulbs, hear the click of fashion photographers' cameras, and the typing of fanzine chatsters. She could see all that happening, once her star was made.

And to think, she told herself in wonder, *it's all going to start with a commercial for Giraldi's Car Corral.*

Chapter 15

Within the hour, Darcy was in position—at her closet. On both shoulders she balanced several outfits, still on their hangers. Strappy shoes dangled from each finger. A different earring dangled from each earlobe, and her neck was aglitter with baubles.

And Lindsay Adams was standing before her, yawning.

"What should I wear?!" Darcy asked her, desperately holding out her bouquet of shoes. "The Manolos or the Jimmy Choos?"

Then she fluttered the gauzy sleeve of one of the dresses on her shoulder.

"The Zac Posen or the Prada?"

Peeking in the mirror at her shiny accessories, she wondered, "Harry Winston or Penny Preville? What should I do?!"

"You," Lindsay pronounced, "should make me lunch."

"Lunch?!" Darcy blurted.

"You said you'd make me lunch if I came over," Lindsay reminded her impatiently.

"We'll get to that," Darcy said, shrugging the clothes off her shoulders and dropping her shoes to the floor. She began pacing her bedroom floor. "But this is so major. This is my acting *debut*. I was about to start taking acting lessons when Mom yanked me out here."

Lindsay seemed unmoved. She stared Darcy down and insisted, "Chicken salad sandwiches. You specifically said there'd be chicken salad sandwiches."

"Okay, okay," Darcy said with a huff, rushing over to her cluttered vanity. She swiped something off it and slapped it into Lindsay's palm.

"Here. This will tide you over."

Lindsay looked at the little tube in her hand.

"This is lip balm!" she protested.

"It's coconut flavored," Darcy said with false enthusiasm. "Mmmmmm!"

Scowling, Lindsay stomped over to Darcy's closet and pointed at a couple random items.

"*That* dress," she declared, "and *those* shoes."

Darcy gasped at the hot-pink frock and kicky cow-boy boots Lindsay had chosen.

Maybe Lindsay was a stylist to the stars in a former life, she marveled. *She's* so *right. That is the perfect ensemble for my television debut!*

"You're a lifesaver," Darcy gushed.

And not to take advantage, but . . .

"Let's move on to accessories."

Over Lindsay's loud sighs of protest, Darcy trotted over to her wardrobe and opened both doors with a dramatic, swooping motion that she hoped was very movie star–like.

She dove into her collection of little purses and big totes, of studded belts and knitted chokers, of sassy bandannas and filmy shawls. Finally, she unearthed the item she'd been looking for—a sixties-era scarf she'd picked up on Melrose Avenue before she'd moved to Bailey. She thought it would provide just the right touch of subtle color. Still scanning the wardrobe, Darcy waved the scarf behind her in Lindsay's general direction.

"What do you think of this scarf?" she inquired.

Thppppptttt!

Lindsay had emitted the loudest, rudest razzberry Darcy had ever heard! She whirled around and shot her friend a shocked look.

"Wow," she said. "Brutally honest."

"It wasn't me!" Lindsay cried. "It was the Baron."

She pointed at Darcy's bed, where the Baron was sitting, cross-legged on top of a pile of Darcy's clothes.

That ape has no respect for my privacy, Darcy groused to herself. *Not to mention my fashion sense! I can't believe he doesn't like this scarf! Surely Lindsay will.*

Darcy held the scarf beneath her chin and batted her eyelashes at Lindsay.

"Soooo?" Darcy prompted.

"The Baron's right," Lindsay said, curling her lip at the scarf's geometric pattern. "That scarf looks like a clown exploded!"

And the next thing Darcy knew? The *Baron* had exploded! Maybe he didn't like Lindsay's snarky tone. Maybe he had a yen for chicken salad, too. Whatever the reason—he suddenly went out of control! He began screeching and jumping up and down on the bed. He waved Darcy's delicate sweaters over his head and cast her favorite jeans onto the floor. He beat his chest and shook his head around and generally acted like the most obnoxious chimpanzee Darcy had ever met! (Okay, he was the *only* chimpanzee Darcy had ever met, but still!)

"Hey, hey!" Darcy yelled, shielding her face from the flying clothes and edging up to her bed. "Chill out!"

She held out her hand to the Baron, who seemed intrigued enough to calm down and grab it. Darcy led the chimp off the bed and sat him in her vanity-table chair.

"You sit here," Darcy ordered, "while we settle on earrings."

The Baron pooched out his lips and looked defiant.

As if he's just gonna sit there because I told him to, Darcy thought, rolling her eyes. *I'm gonna have to do better than that.*

Darcy scanned her bedroom, looking for a solution among the piles of clothes.

Aha! She had a *Folks* magazine on her nightstand. The Baron *did* love periodicals! Darcy swooped up the glossy gossip mag and plunked it into the Baron's lap.

"You can read this," she told him. "I'm sure Britney's up to something wacky."

As Darcy headed to her jewelry chest on top of her dresser, Lindsay glanced at her watch.

"Listen, Darcy," she said. "We gotta get back to

work. We need to finish stocking those shelves, there are vaccines to put away, somebody's got to make chicken salad sandwiches. . . ."

"Oh," Darcy said, biting her lip. She *so* couldn't go back to work yet! Not when her commercial outfit was so woefully unaccessorized! But she also couldn't bail on Lindsay. When Lindsay got hungry, she got cranky! Crank*ier*, that was.

"Um . . ." Darcy hemmed. "Well, maybe I can bring some earrings to work and keep thinking."

"You're not gonna have time for that!" Lindsay insisted. "We have *a lot* of work to do this afternoon."

"Right. Okay," Darcy said with a sigh. "You're right."

Still, she couldn't resist sneaking just a *few* options into her purse and jeans pockets.

It's just a half-dozen pairs of earrings, three scarves, and a necklace or three, Darcy told herself guiltily. *It's not like they're going to distract me from work for more than a few minutes.*

Speaking of distractions, the Baron was—fishily— *not* one at the moment! After stuffing one more bauble into her pocket, Darcy glanced at her vanity to see what he was up to.

Into was more like it! The Baron had totally raided her makeup drawer. His lips were coated in Darcy's favorite pink lipstick! And over his eyes, he'd put on Darcy's best Jackie O–style sunglasses.

"Hey!" Darcy squealed. "What are you doing?"

The Baron, of course, responded with nothing but a smirk and another rude noise.

And Lindsay? *She* was grinning. *She* thought this was all very funny!

"Well," Lindsay quipped, "we know who can help pick your makeup!"

"Har, har," Darcy fumed. She was just stepping toward the bad, bad Baron to snatch back her stuff when the chimp hopped off her chair. Then he swiped a plastic cosmetic case off her vanity. And this wasn't just *any* cosmetic case. This was her precious Lip Gloss Caboodle. Inside that case was Darcy's prized collection of lip glosses. We're talking squeezable tubes, sponge-tipped wands, strawberry Lip Smackers—everything a girl could want for her lips! Darcy had been amassing this collection since the sixth grade, and she wasn't about to let the Baron smear it all over his chimpy lips.

Yeah, but try telling that to the Baron! As Darcy gasped in horror and lunged to grab her Caboodle from his hands, the chimp made a run for it!

Chapter 16

Wild Wisdom . . . *The upper shell of the tortoise or turtle is composed of about fifty bones.*

Victoria Fields couldn't have been happier. She was on her knees in the good, honest earth, tending to her vegetable garden with her trusty sidekicks, Eli and Jack. The sun was warm on her back, the air was filled with the sweet fragrances of the farm, and Hollywood was just a distant memory.

How on earth, Victoria thought with a happy sigh, *could anyone find the red carpet more appealing than these red tomatoes?*

Plucking a big, ripe one off its vine, Victoria admired its plump beauty.

"I can't get over how well all the tomatoes are coming in!" she gushed to Eli. "As shiny and red as my Uncle Trevor's nose."

Eli smiled and nodded as he put all of the toma-

toes he'd picked into a bushel basket. Victoria supposed she should put her tomato into the basket, too,
but she just couldn't. The warm, red globe in her
hand was too luscious not to eat right then. As she
brought the juicy fruit to her mouth, she thought,
*Any star can have foie gras at the Four Seasons and lar-
doons at Le Cirque. But how many of them get to eat
their own homegrown, freshly plucked tomatoes?*

Victoria had just closed her eyes and gotten ready
to bite the tomato when Eli made an observation
about the fabulous fruits.

"Usually, the raccoons eat the tomatoes," he pointed out, "but I sprinkled some stuff on them to keep
them away."

"Oh?" Victoria said, pausing before she sunk her
teeth into her snack. She was always eager to learn
more about the workings of her farm. "What?"

"Crystallized wolf urine," Eli said with a matter-
of-fact nod of his shaggy head. "The only problem is,
it makes the tomatoes taste like wolf tinkle."

"Well!" Victoria blurted. She threw the lovely
thing over her shoulder and dusted the dirt off her
hands. *"That's* too bad."

"You know what else would be too bad?" Jack said
with a rasp. He was leaning on the garden fence, look-

ing glum. "If Kathi Giraldi's dad's car dealership's commercial didn't have a big movie star in it."

"Jack," Victoria said with a sigh, folding up her gardening gloves and stuffing them into her jeans pocket. "We've been through this. I have no interest in acting again. I've lived that life."

"Well, I haven't!" Jack yelled. "And I *want to!*"

He shook his fists at the sky melodramatically.

Jack actually would do quite well in the movie business, Victoria realized. *He's hyperactive and hyperbolic. He's a fantastic wheeler-dealer, completely willing to double-cross my daughter. He's as Hollywood as a young boy can be! But I think I'll just keep that information to myself until Jack's at least eighteen.*

What she *did* tell Jack was a big, fat no.

"Look," she insisted, "even if I wanted to act again, this commercial means the world to Darcy. I couldn't take that away from her."

"Sure you can!" Jack scoffed. "Happens all the time."

"Jack, it would break Darcy's heart," Victoria said, smiling as she pictured her daughter's pretty, soft smile, her twinkly blue eyes, her gently blushing cheeks. "She's a very delicate, sensitive girl."

"You stinking, flea-bitten hair bag!"

Victoria gasped and jumped to her feet.

Who on earth is that? she thought. *It must be some neighbor I haven't met yet. Nobody I know would ever screech and carry on like tha—oh, my.*

Yup. Victoria had just spotted the source of the screech. It was her "delicate, sensitive" daughter, Darcy, and she was chasing after Baron von Chimpie! The Baron was clutching some sort of makeup case and scampering just out of Darcy's reach.

"Get back here!" Darcy insisted, "or I'll turn you into monkey chow!"

The Baron, of course, paid no heed and darted into the garden. Darcy skidded to a halt between a couple of rows of tomatoes and glared at the chimp. Behind her, Lindsay trotted up. She looked like she was trying hard not to laugh.

"You know," Eli pointed out to Victoria's enraged daughter, "he's not really a monkey. Chimps are from the ape family."

"Well, monkey's more fun to say," Darcy retorted, flipping an unraveling French braid over her shoulder, "so I'm saying monkey."

Then she scowled harder, took a threatening step toward the Baron, and held out both hands.

"Give me that back!" she demanded. "I'm warning you."

"*Eeeeee!*"

Screeching, the Baron stashed Darcy's case beneath one arm and used the other arm to dart into the thickest thatch of tomato vines. He stuck his tongue out at Darcy and shook his head hard.

Victoria shook her head, too, though not hard enough to muss her blond 'do. Standing between the chimpanzee and Darcy, she admonished her daughter.

"Now, now, Darcy," she said. "Don't threaten the Baron."

"But he's a thief!" Darcy cried, pointing at the Baron in outrage.

Oh, my, Victoria thought again. *Now I can see why Darcy's so desperate to get her cosmetic case back. Her fingernails look like they've been gnawed by a beaver! I'm sure if the Baron realizes that Darcy's in the throes of a manicure emergency, he'll change his mischievous ways. Now then . . .*

Victoria placed a placating—if slightly dirt-smudged—hand on Darcy's shoulder and said, "I'm sure it's just a misunderstanding."

Then she turned to the cowering chimp and said in the sweetest way possible, "Baron? May I please have the makeup?"

Baron von Chimpie hung his head for a moment,

looking longingly at the sparkly, pink box in his hands. But then he did the right thing and handed the box over. Victoria promptly passed it on to Darcy.

"There, see?" Victoria said proudly. "If we all remain calm, everything's fine."

Splat!

"Oh!" Victoria screamed. Something warm and slimy and redolent of . . . *crystallized wolf urine* was sliding down her swanlike neck! Stunned and horrified, Victoria whirled around to face the Baron.

Not *only* was her former costar *completely* unrepentant for pelting her with a ripe tomato, he was holding another one in his hand! And he was rearing back to throw it!

This didn't seem to bother Jack much. He was too busy making fun of Victoria. Running up to get a closer look at the besmirched star, he began giggling wildly.

"Ha-ha-ha!" he crowed, pointing at Victoria's slimy face. "Pretty good aim for a chimp!"

Splat!

Jack's grin turned into a very shocked *O*. Now the Baron had nailed *him*! And *his* tomato had been extra ripe. It had exploded on impact, coating his entire head in goop and seeds.

Pretty good aim indeed, Victoria chortled to herself. But oh, the Baron was just getting started. The next time Victoria glanced his way, the chimp was holding tomatoes in both hands *and* in one of his prehensile feet!

"The chimp's going nuts!" Eli screamed. "Everybody run!"

Eli made a dash for the garden gate. Of course, a squash vine got in his way, and he tripped.

"Oh, man!" he cried.

The Baron moved in for the splat, pelting Eli with all three of his tomatoes. Then he quickly turned to pluck up more ammo.

Darcy screamed.

Victoria shouted.

Jack shrieked like a girl.

Lindsay was too sensible to scream. She simply ran. The others scrambled after her, but in the end, nobody was quicker than the Baron. By the time they'd made it into the house, they were all gross with tomato guts.

Once upon a time, Baron von Chimpie had been Victoria's friend. On their movie set, Victoria would steal bananas from the craft services table and slip them to the Baron. The Baron, in turn, would engage Victoria in endless games of tic-tac-toe. They had run lines together and read each other tidbits from the newspaper. They'd treated each other with complete mutual respect.

Now, Victoria realized with distress, it was out-and-out ape vs. ex-movie star *war*!

Chapter 17

Darcy and Lindsay made it back to Creature Comforts way late, what with the tomato onslaught and all. Immediately, they dove into their work. Lindsay snatched up the price-tag gun and began clicking stickers onto cans of pet food.

Darcy, of course, began practicing her poses. First, she did her Vanna White flourish, the kind she'd mastered to introduce her mother to TV reporters on the red carpet.

But then she realized, *Hey, wait a minute. That move has so been done. It's been seen on* Entertainment This Evening *and* Yo! Entertainment. *It even made the "Fashion Do" list in* Folks *magazine. I have to come up with something new! Right now!*

Darcy closed her eyes and took a deep breath. She cleansed her mind and tried to visualize her motivation.

Superloaded 4x4, she thought dreamily. *Extended cab pickup with seat warmers and a dozen cup holders. A frosty green SUV with pink racing stripes. And a driver's license!*

Darcy's eyes snapped open, and her hands swooped to the side, her fingers fluttering. Meanwhile, she raised her eyebrows and opened her mouth in a delighted grin. Yes! She had it. Now she just had to practice the move a hundred times or so to get it *just* righ—

"What are you doing?"

Darcy stopped in mid arm-swoop and glanced at Lindsay behind the Creature Comforts counter. Her fists were on her hips, and she was looking at Darcy with a scowl.

"I'm . . . practicing for the commercial," Darcy said. Before Lindsay could dis her, she decided to wow her with her moves. Launching into her arm-swoop, she beamed at Lindsay and chirped, "Take it from me—if you want glamour, there's nothing like this three-quarter-ton pickup. I'd drive *this* to a Hollywood premiere!"

Darcy relaxed and gave Lindsay an expectant look.

Does she love it? she thought needily. *Does she hate it? Does she* really *think my scarf looks like a detonated clown?*

Apparently the answer was: d) none of the above. Otherwise known as, "I don't care!"

"Look," Lindsay ordered Darcy, "practice for your commercial on your own time. We've got work to do here. It only makes it harder that I still smell like tomatoes. You're supposed to use tomato juice to get rid of skunk smell, but nobody tells you how to get rid of tomato smell!"

Okay, I've just learned something, Darcy thought. *A tomatoey Lindsay is even crankier than a hungry Lindsay! Better appease. . . .*

"You're right," Darcy conceded. "Sorry."

Nodding curtly, Lindsay affixed the last pet-food price tag and began unpacking a box of turtle supplies. Darcy went to the shop's avian section and heaved a bag of birdseed onto a shelf. The bag was so heavy, she found herself angling her body backward to keep her balance.

Hey, wait a minute, Darcy thought. *That move may have been accidental, but it was also good!*

Darcy leaned backward again, cocking one hip out jauntily. This time, instead of tossing birdseed onto the shelf, she did her arm-swoop. Perfect! Now Darcy had another classic move for her commercial.

She tried it again. *Lean-swoop-grin.*

And again. *Lean-swoop-grin . . . and wink!*

Ooh, Darcy thought, another brilliant addition. Lemme try that agai—

"Darcy!"

Lindsay was fully glaring at Darcy now. If she hadn't looked so mad, Darcy would have giggled at the goofy turtle toys Lindsay was clutching in each fist.

But, of course, she *was* that mad.

"I am *not* going to do all of this myself," Lindsay sputtered. "Now, come on!"

Now it was Darcy who began to feel a bit miffed. She was starting to wonder if Lindsay really knew how incredibly important this commercial was!

I mean, it's not just my up-and-coming acting career on the line here, Darcy told herself. *It's also Mr. Giraldi and all his unsold cars and trucks. Not to mention Kathi! Without me, she may never have Paris! (Okay, maybe a girl can live without ever seeing Paris, Texas, but still. . . .)*

Darcy frowned at Lindsay and grabbed some birdseed.

113

"I'm doing it," she defended herself, just a bit sullenly. "I'm multitasking. Sheesh!"

As much as Darcy had come to like her job at Creature Comforts—well, as long as she didn't have to deal with reptiles—she was relieved when her shift was over and she could come home to the farm. While she'd been at work, her mom and Eli had cleaned up all the tomato goop.

Now, Darcy and Victoria were relaxing in a most movie-star manner—on the farmhouse's front porch, sipping cool, pink lemonade.

"So, for the commercial," Darcy announced to her mother breathlessly, "I'm trying to decide if I want to do an accent."

Again, Darcy closed her eyes to seek out her motivation. She pictured a passionate, raven-haired girl, the daughter perhaps of an Italian countess and a Scottish race-car driver. Someone who was refined, but could appreciate an eight-valve engine that could go from zero to sixty in six seconds flat.

"Ey!" Darcy said in her loud TV voice. "Atsa barrgreen fera carrrrrr!"

Oooh, Darcy thought. *That was my best rolled* R *ever. All this rehearsal is really helping!*

She looked eagerly to her mom for feedback.

Victoria seemed to be having trouble swallowing her lemonade. That must have been why her face looked so pained. When she finally found her voice, she said, "Why don't you keep thinking about that one?"

"Really?" Darcy said. "Cuz—"

"*Buenos días, muchachas!* That means '*Aloha, señoritas.*'"

Darcy turned to see who'd interrupted her and gasped. It was the Brennan brothers! They were waving at the Fields women from the base of the porch steps. They looked dapper in their all-white Spanish outfits, complete with red neckerchiefs. They also looked, er, injured! Brett's arm was in a sling, and Brandon's neck was in a brace!

"We're back from the Running of the Bulls," Brandon said with a big grin.

"It looks like the bulls ran over you!" Victoria cried.

"Nope!" Brett said with a guileless smile. "I fell off the escalator at the airport."

"Then *he* fell on *me*," Brandon said with equal cheer. "*Whomp!*"

"So," Brett said, motioning at the door with his

non-broken arm. "How's that chimp of ours?"

Victoria got to her feet and beckoned the brothers and Darcy into the house. As they made their way through the kitchen, Victoria said carefully, "Well, the truth about the Baron is, he's a bit of a handful."

"A handful?" Darcy scoffed. "He's an earthquake with thumbs on his feet!"

"Truth is," Brett admitted, "since we got him, he's been nothing but hairy, angry monkey-trouble!"

"That's so odd," Victoria said with a frown. "He was such a pussycat when we worked on *Death Knocks at Midnight*. He brought me tea and a newspaper every morning!"

"Well, all he's brought us is trouble," Brett said. "If he doesn't get better, I'm afraid we'll have to find someone else to take care of him."

Up to that point, Darcy had been only half-listening to all this Baron talk. The other half of her had been envisioning her commercial. She'd been considering adding a little cancan kick to her routine. But when Brett threatened to ship the Baron off, it made Darcy wake up and forget about her commercial. (Well, for a moment.) She butted into the adults' conversation.

"You'd get rid of him?" she asked Brett fearfully.

I mean, the Baron and I have our issues, Darcy

thought, *but it's not like I want to see him banished!*

"Oh, I'm sure that won't be necessary," Victoria reassured them all as they headed into the living room. "He's probably just adjusting."

"Yeah," Darcy chimed in. "He's really not that bad!"

With one look at the living room, though, Darcy had to correct herself on that one.

"He's horrible!"

Chapter 18

Wild Wisdom . . . *The American Humane Association was given the rights to set guidelines for animal actors in 1940, but the right was revoked in 1966. In 1980, they regained sole authority to protect animals used in film and television.*

Darcy couldn't believe how much havoc one little chimpanzee had been able to wreak in the past half hour! Every pillow was tossed off of every piece of furniture. The walls? They were scribbled with crayons! There were banana and orange peels everywhere. And the chandelier was draped with toilet paper that fluttered through the air as the light fixture swung back and forth.

And why was the chandelier doing this crazy dance? Because Baron von Chimpie was hanging off of it! Talk about a jungle gym.

The worst part of this scene of destruction was Eli. The poor guy was lashed with rope to a wooden post in the center of the room. On top of his head was an apple. Tossed onto the floor nearby was a bow and arrow! The Baron had been using the Fields' handy-boy for target practice! Luckily, the chimp was clearly a poor shot. There were pockmarks all over the walls and floors, but thankfully Eli and his apple were unharmed.

Which wasn't to say that Eli wasn't *freaked out*. When he saw Darcy, Victoria, and the Brennans, he almost burst into tears.

"Help . . . me!" he said with a rasp.

So they did. They untied Eli, who was so shaken up, he immediately headed home to his own farm. Then the Brennans, Darcy, and her mom gathered up the naughty chimp and took him directly to Creature Comforts. Kevin wasn't dealing with any skinny snakes or pregnant pigs, so he was able to see the Baron immediately.

As Darcy and the grown-ups hovered anxiously around the Baron on the examining table, Kevin tapped lightly on the chimp's chest and listened to his back with a stethoscope. He peeked into the Baron's ears and stared into his eyes. Finally, he took out a tongue depressor and said, "Okay, Baron, say ah!"

Obediently, the Baron stuck out his tongue and opened wide for the vet.

"Ahhhhhh," Kevin growled sympathetically as he peered down the Baron's throat. After a good, long look, he tossed the tongue depressor into the trash, got to his feet, and shrugged.

"Well, there's nothing physically wrong with him that you couldn't cure with a breath mint," he declared. "A breath mint the size of a school bus!"

"Then how did such a delightful chimp become such a delinquent?" Victoria wondered.

"Probably watching violent cartoons," Darcy said with a knowing frown. "That's how it usually starts."

Brett and Brandon nodded sorrowfully.

"I suspect it's psychological," Kevin offered. "I'd say he's acting out because he's bored."

"Why would he be bored?" Darcy asked. "He's not stuck in a cage or anything."

Kevin looked thoughtful.

"I treated a highly trained show-jumping horse once," he said. "After he was retired, he didn't have his task anymore, and he got bored and frustrated."

Darcy nudged her mom with her elbow.

"Like Grandpa, when he retired," she said.

"Yes," Victoria agreed. "But he eventually snapped out of it."

"How'd he do that?" Brett asked.

"He married his twenty-six-year-old yoga teacher," Darcy said with a shrug. "Bought a sailboat and went to Tahiti. Surprised the heck out of my grandmother!"

A moment of awkward silence followed.

Whoops, Darcy thought. *TMI?*

Luckily, Kevin brought the chat back to practical matters.

"I'm not sure Baron von Chimpie needs a trophy wife to cheer him up," he said. "Just some simple chores might help him feel useful."

Darcy rolled her eyes and let out a long-suffering sigh. She *so* needed to blog about that one. Slipping her PDA out of her jeans pocket, she scribbled a quick post.

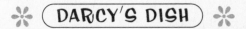

❋ (DARCY'S DISH) ❋

I don't know what it is about this place, folks. Their answer for everything is "do chores." What ever happened to "go shopping"?!

Victoria, on the other hand, was all whistle-while-you-work on the matter.

"I'm sure," she said brightly, "I could find some things for him to do around the house."

"When he's done at your house, could you send him over here?"

That was Lindsay. She had just walked into the exam room lugging a heavy box of supplies. As she crossed the room to empty the jars and bottles onto a shelf above the exam table, she gave Darcy a resentful glare and added, "I could use some *help* around here."

Darcy was taken aback.

"What's that supposed to mean?" she said.

"It means," Lindsay complained, "you're supposed to help me with inventory, and I've been stuck doing the whole thing myself! I was here till nine o'clock!"

"Hey!" Darcy said huffily. "This commercial wasn't my idea!"

Everybody in the room—even the Baron!—gave Darcy a skeptical look.

"Well . . . okay, it *was* my idea," Darcy allowed with an eye roll. "But it was Kathi who wanted me in it! And I don't let my friends down."

"Oh, I guess I don't count as a friend," Lindsay said quietly as her cheeks went bright red. "Just a coworker."

Wait a minute, Darcy thought. *That's not what I said, is it?!*

Lindsay didn't give Darcy a chance to contradict

her out loud. She turned her attention to her dad and announced, "I'll be out doing my job."

She gave Darcy a cold look and added, "*And* Darcy's."

Chapter 19

Wild Wisdom . . . *Goldfish lose their color if they are kept in dim light or are placed in a body of running water.*

Okay, Darcy wanted to help Lindsay out and everything? But: A) She didn't really appreciate being *humiliated* by Lindsay in front of *everybody*. And: B) She had another job to do. She had to help her mom devise some cheer-inducing chores for the bored Baron.

They started with apple-picking. Not only was it a fun *and* delicious activity, it was tailor-made for the chimpanzee. While Darcy, Eli, and Victoria plucked the apples off the lowest branches, the Baron could shimmy up to the treetops to get at the most sun-soaked fruits.

And that's exactly what he did. It wasn't long before the Baron was standing before an entire bushel basket of apples he'd picked himself.

Between plucking their own apples, Darcy and Eli glanced at each other and raised their eyebrows.

Huh! Maybe this whole "doing chores" thing isn't *just bogus pop psychology,* Darcy had to admit to herself as she moved onto the next, fruit-heavy tree. *The Baron seems happy. Productive. Downright peaceful! Kevin's idea is working alrea—*

Splunk!

Mid-muse, Darcy was startled by a weird noise— something between a *splat* and a *thunk*. Pausing in her apple-picking, she looked around.

Splunk!

There it was again! Except this time, it was followed by a loud "Ow!"

Dashing back to Eli's tree, Darcy found him rubbing his back, a pained wince on his face.

Splunk!

Eli jumped and whirled around. The Baron grinned and dipped into his basket of apples. After he'd succeeded in pelting Eli with three of 'em, it looked as if he was going for a fourth!

I guess tomatoes and apples really make the Baron see red! Darcy realized.

After that, the Baron started going full steam. He hit Eli yet again, just missed Victoria's head with

another apple, and finally took aim at Darcy! She ran!
But not as fast as Eli and her mom!

Expelled from the garden due to an apple, Darcy
complained to herself as the trio darted for shelter. *A
familiar story* and *a total bummer!*

After that, Eli suggested they plant some tree
seedlings that had just arrived.

"Oh, no," Darcy protested. "No more fruit. The
Baron cannot be trusted around it!"

But when Eli promised her that these trees were
crape myrtles—all flowers, no fruit—she consented.

And again, the chore got off to a great start. The
three humans and the chimp did a stellar job planting
the first tree. After they anchored it in a nice little
mound of dirt, they moved on to the next one. Eli
dug. Victoria and Darcy shoveled earth. And the
Baron . . . hey, where did the Baron go?

Mrrrrrrrrr!

Darcy cocked an ear.

*That sounds just like the new lawn tractor Mom
bought for our meadow,* she thought. *But if Eli's standing right here, who's driving it?*

"Ahhhh!" Victoria screamed, pointing at the other
side of the lawn.

Oh. The *Baron* was driving the lawn tractor. He was driving it right at the three unhappy farmers!

Once again, they ran for their lives while the chimp chased after them, steering the tractor like a pro and screeching with angry abandon.

Okay, Darcy thought next. *We've gotta find something low-tech. No gardening. No driving. Something soothing and creative . . . I've got it! The Ralph Lauren paint I ordered just came in yesterday. We can paint our back shed the color of a New England robin's egg.*

Outfitted with four paint rollers, Darcy, Eli, Victoria, and the Baron got to work. They painted in silence, but for the birds chirping and the rhythmic *squish-squish* of their sponge rollers. Even Darcy was enjoying the labor. She got so in the work-zone, in fact, that she went several minutes without checking on the Baron.

When she did, she gasped in shock! But for once, the surprise was a pleasant one! Not only was the Baron *not* causing mayhem or personal injury to Eli, he was painting a beautiful self-portrait. In his picture, the Baron looked pensive and soulful. Darcy was so impressed, she nudged Eli and pointed at the painting.

"Whoa!" Eli whispered.

He continued painting his section of the shed wall as he admired the Baron's work. Until suddenly, Eli uttered an "Oh, man!"

Darcy looked at Eli and suppressed a laugh. While he'd been gazing upon the Baron's artistry, Eli had run his paint roller right over his own hand.

Guess I better revise that "no personal injury to Eli" part, Darcy thought with a quiet giggle. *He's gonna spend the rest of the day with a robin's egg blue mani!*

It was Eli who then decided everyone should head indoors to work. Housework, he said, would be safer.

While Darcy dusted the awards on the fireplace mantel, Victoria washed windows and Eli folded laundry. The Baron's job was skimming beneath the sofa cushions with the vacuum cleaner's long tube attachment. He was doing great until . . .

Ripppp!

Darcy spun around to see Eli wearing a shocked look and—nothing but his undershirt!

Just behind him was the Baron. The chimp was waving his vacuum tube in the air, just as it inhaled the last of Eli's plaid flannel! The Baron had sucked the shirt right off of Eli's back!

And in the end, none of their death-defying chores even worked. That night, as a pooped Darcy and Victoria made themselves a simple dinner, they glanced into the living room. The chimp was staring out the window, his hand flung dramatically across his forehead.

The Baron was still bored. And where he'd aim his next destructive impulse, Darcy could only guess!

Chapter 20

Wild Wisdom . . . *The placement of a donkey's eyes in its head enables it to see all four of its feet at all times.*

Darcy would have been really worried about the Baron—if she didn't have a commercial to shoot. But have a commercial to shoot she did, the very next day.

Ever the consummate professional, Darcy showed up on the set (otherwise known as Giraldi's Car Corral) on time and already decked out in her Acting-Debut Outfit. She wore her kicky pink cowboy boots and hot-pink cowboy dress, complete with little puffed sleeves and a ruffle at the hem. To top the ensemble off right, Darcy had chosen a lime green cowboy hat worn low over her carefully curled hair.

The only thing she lacked on her big day was a proper entourage. Instead of a band of sycophants, managers, agents, and personal trainers tailing her every step, she had, er, her mom. And Jack. But *he*

barely counted. In fact, he was shooting Darcy dark looks as she pulled Victoria aside and asked her to go over her script with her.

"I thought Lindsay was going to run lines with you," Victoria said, looking confused.

"She's mad at me!" Darcy blurted with an indignant eye roll. "Apparently, if *I'm* not gonna help her, *she's* not gonna help me."

"Ah," Victoria said cryptically. She gave Darcy a squinty look, but Darcy chalked it off to the superbright sun and returned to the subject of her commercial.

"Anyway," she burbled, "I'm afraid my dialogue is a little dull. Do you think it's okay to spice it up a little?"

"Sure," Victoria said. "I used to change my lines all the time! Writers *love* that."

Darcy nodded and said, "I was thinking of some choreography."

Then she launched into the cancan kick she'd envisioned the day before. As she bounced and kicked and twisted and kicked and bounced some more, she huffed out her lines: "That's right! You can afford our easy terms. Ten percent down. Low monthly payments with competitive interest rates. . . ."

Victoria had another mysterious look on her face—something between pride and indigestion. At least, that's how she looked until Jack swooped in, grabbed her elbow, and whisked her to the edge of the set.

"Last chance, sweetheart," he rasped to the former movie star. "It's not too late to give Darcy the old heave-ho and get you into this thing."

Darcy's mouth dropped open.

Why that little double-crosser! she thought. *He's trying to get my own mother to stab me in the back. I mean, sure that happens all the time in Hollywood, but we don't* live *in Hollywood anymore. We live in Bailey, where we have simple values, simple pleas—wait a minute! What am I saying?*

Darcy was so stunned to find herself quoting her mother's Bailey propaganda that she couldn't summon the wit to cut Jack off. Instead, she plopped herself down in her director's chair, pretended to read her script, and eavesdropped.

"Jack," her mom was saying. "I sai—"

"This isn't about me anymore," Jack interrupted desperately. "This is about all those kids out there who are growing up in a world without Victoria Fields."

Victoria nodded cynically, but Jack pressed on, putting a hand to his heart and looking into the distance. His eyes even looked a little moist!

Whoa, lay it on a little thick, why don't ya? Darcy thought.

"Don't do this for me," Jack begged Victoria. "Do it for the children."

Victoria thought for a moment longer, and then nodded crisply.

"Very well," she announced, "I'll do it!"

What?!?!

Again, Darcy was so stunned, she couldn't move. She couldn't speak! Whatever happened to simple values and simple pleasures?!

"But, like any big star," Victoria went on, "I have some requirements. I'll need fresh fruit in my dressing room."

"Not a problem," Jack said. He turned and marched over to a cluster of crew members. The commercial's director (usually known as the custodian at the local farm-news station) was about to chomp down on an apple when Jack snatched it out of his hand.

"Thanks, chief," Jack said to the flummoxed guy. "Catch ya later."

Skimming back over to Victoria, Jack plunked the apple into her hand and said, "Voilà! Fresh fruit."

Victoria shook her head and handed it back.

"I require a tropical platter," she corrected Jack. "Fresh guava, papaya, and Hawaiian star fruit. I am after all, a star!"

But . . . but Mom hates papaya, Darcy sputtered inwardly. *She always says the smell reminds her of old silk shoes. Why would she ask for that?*

Suddenly Darcy's mouth—which had been hanging open during Jack and Victoria's entire exchange—clamped shut. And then it curved into a sly smile. She'd suddenly figured out *exactly* what her mom was doing.

Let's just say, Darcy thought with a giggle, *that for every trick Jack Adams has up his sleeve, my movie-star mom has two.*

Speaking of Jack Adams, the squirt was looking a little taken aback by the whole tropical fruit platter concept.

"Um, well," he was saying to Victoria. But again, she cut him off.

"I'll need an air-conditioned trailer," she informed him.

"My dad's got a fan," Jack shrugged. "I could put

some ice cubes in front of it."

"The trailer," Victoria waxed on, "shall have a physical trainer and a licensed astrologist. I need three personal golf carts, each with an Italian-born driver . . ."

"Um," Jack squeaked.

Darcy had to hide another giggle. She could see the sweat on Jack's brow from several feet away.

"Now, then," Victoria continued breezily, while Jack began to have a minor meltdown, "let's talk private helicopters . . ."

Chapter 21

Wild Wisdom . . . *Cats cannot survive on a vegetarian diet.*

While Darcy was making her last preparations for her acting debut, Lindsay was hard at work at Creature Comforts. She was transferring cattle feed from a giant burlap bag into a giant barrel. The task seemed so, well, giant that Lindsay couldn't help but sigh as she scooped up the grassy-smelling pellets.

Scoop.

Sigh.

Hope Darcy's enjoying herself out in the sunshine, Lindsay grumbled to herself.

Scoop.

Sigh.

This would be so *much easier if I weren't doing it all myself,* Lindsay thought. *But I guess you really can't count on people. One day, you're friends; the next, you're*

just coworkers. And at the moment, Darcy and I are barely even coworkers! Her little car commercial seems to matter so much more than the health and welfare of Bailey's animal kingdo—

"Heya, honey!"

Lindsay jumped, just catching herself from spilling a scoopful of feed all over the floor. She'd been so busy grumbling to herself, she hadn't even heard her dad emerge from the clinic. As usual, he was cradling a critter in his arms—a fuzzy, young tabby cat.

"How come you aren't out watching them make the big commercial?" Kevin asked.

"Because somebody has to do Darcy's work," Lindsay sulked as she returned to her scooping. "*She* sure isn't doing it."

"Ahh," her dad said, nodding sagely. Giving the kitty's head a pat, he cocked his head and announced, "You know, Darcy's very much like Baron von Chimpie."

Okay, *that* made Lindsay finally stop working.

What?! she thought. *I know some of the things that Dad says are seriously out of left field. But comparing Darcy to a chimpanzee? That's out of outer space!*

On the other hand, she realized, *as peeved as I am at Darcy right now, it's sort of satisfying to compare her to a rambunctious ape who smells like funky bananas.*

Raising one eyebrow at her sweet but addled father, Lindsay said, "Okay, go."

"Darcy and the Baron have both been taken away from their normal life," Kevin pointed out. "Darcy's a long way from Malibu. It doesn't matter if you're a performing chimp or a movie-star's daughter—when your life changes, you react."

"So," Lindsay queried, "if Darcy was a professional chimp, I'd *still* be doing her work?"

Kevin grimaced and gazed at the ceiling.

"Darn," he muttered. "I never seem to get these lessons right."

Lindsay chuckled. Whenever she was bummed, she could always count on her dad to inadvertently cheer her up. He *did* mean well. He just didn't get people nearly as much as he did animals!

"The point is," Kevin went on, "if she's a friend of yours, maybe you should consider what Darcy's going through."

Lindsay blinked.

Now that *made sense,* she thought with a twinge

of guilt. *It was even pretty astute! I mean, for my dad. I should put myself in Darcy's shoes. How would I feel if I had to leave behind Bailey and Creature Comforts for, say, Beverly Hills? Where there's nothing to do but shop and get icky sea-mud body wraps with cucumbers on my eyes? Bo-ring!*

Lindsay looked down at the feed scoop in her hands and murmured, "Maybe I should cut Darcy some slack."

"No, don't!" Kevin cried.

Lindsay looked up at her dad in confusion. He looked all twisty and his face wore a gruesome grimace!

"It was . . . just a thought," Lindsay said hesitantly.

"No, it's the cat," Kevin explained with a grunt. "I forgot to trim her back claws. They're digging into me. Ouch!"

Kevin hurried into the clinic to the tune of the cat's mischievous meows.

Left alone in the shop (well, except for the old guy who perpetually snoozed on the bench beneath the window) Lindsay put her scoop down on the counter and walked to the screen door. Crossing her arms over her chest, she gazed across the gloom of the front porch into the brilliant sunshine.

Well, that was an enlightening chat, she thought. *The only question now is—what do I do with this new-found enlightenment?*

Chapter 22

Wild Wisdom . . . *Chimpanzees do not swim.*

Back at Giraldi's Car Corr—*er, ahem,* the set,
Victoria was *still* issuing her list of demands to Jack.
And Darcy was still spying on them, giggling behind her
script.

This might be Mom's best performance yet! she
thought.

"At three o'clock," Victoria was saying, "I break for
tea. Served by Orlando Bloom."

Jack slapped his palm to his forehead and shook his
fists at the heavens.

I don't think he can take much more of this, Darcy
predicted.

"My dressing room will be decorated in silk bro-
cade," Victoria said, sweeping an arm out dramatically.
"It will feature tame peacocks and a Shiatsu masseuse."

"Um, I think we should save some of this stuff," Jack squeaked, "for when you get back to Hollywood."

"But I want it now," Victoria whined. "Now! Do you hear?"

"Well, I can't get it for you now," Jack sputtered. "You're out of control!"

With that, he gave up altogether. He spun around wildly and began running! As he whizzed past Darcy's director's chair, he blurted at her, "Watch out for your mom. She's nuts!"

As Jack dashed away, Victoria caught Darcy's eye and shot her a wink.

Darcy gave her mom a big grin and a thumbs-up.

No backstabber, my mom! she thought proudly. *This almost makes me forgive her for making me pack up and move to Bailey. Whatever happens, I know I can count on Victoria Fields: mom first, movie star second.*

"You look good."

Darcy blinked. Lindsay had appeared next to her director's chair. And she'd . . . actually given Darcy a compliment?

Totally confused, Darcy said, "What are you doing here? I thought you were all mad at me."

"Well, I kinda was," Lindsay admitted, thrusting

her hands into her pants pockets. "But . . . the thing is, you're exactly like the chimp."

Okay, my little truce with Baron von Chimpie aside, Darcy thought, *I really hope Lindsay's not implying that I smell like a funky banana.*

To Lindsay, she sputtered, "And . . . thank you?"

"You got pulled away from your Hollywood life," Lindsay explained, "so you're all weirded out. And if dressing up like a saloon chick and trying to sell a used pickup helps you deal, then I support that."

Darcy grinned at Lindsay. She had to totally resist giving her bud a grateful hug. Lindsay was not a huggy kind of girl. So instead, Darcy just gave Lindsay a big grin and said, "Thanks!"

The sweet moment left Darcy totally gooey, but there was no time to bathe in the good vibes. The commercial's director was approaching her chair.

"Uh . . . Darcy?" he said nervously. "We're ready for rehearsal. And, er, will you let me know if I'm doing anything wrong? I've never really directed before. I'm mostly in charge of the 'Technical Difficulties, Please Stand By' slide at the farm-news station."

"You'll be great," Darcy said graciously. She'd learned from her mom to *always* be gracious with film crews.

Taking a deep breath, Darcy stood up and marched to her position. She was standing in front of a row of shiny vehicles with their low, low prices painted onto their windshields. Above her head flapped a string of triangular flags. And as Darcy gazed into the camera lens, she felt certain that she was staring down her very destiny!

Until, that was, she was totally distracted by a visitor to the set. Make that three: Brett, Brandon, and the Baron were ambling up to Victoria, who was standing on the sidelines to watch the filming. When the Baron tugged at her skirt hem, Victoria looked down at him and smiled.

"Ah!" she said to the brothers. "Bringing the Baron down for a little visit?"

"Naw," Brett said with a long face. "We're just stopping by so he can say so long."

"*And* we heard there were free corn dogs here," Brandon added.

The Baron was looking down at his long toes and pooching his lips out into a silent razzberry.

What?! Darcy thought. *Where's the Baron going? And why does he have to do it during my commercial?*

Victoria frowned, too.

"Baron von Chimpie's going away?" she said.

"We just can't handle him," Brett sighed. "But he'll be okay. He's going to a primate rescue shelter."

Clearly trying to cheer the chimp up, Brett leaned down and offered, "Want a corn dog?"

The Baron shook his head and looked away, as moody as Shakespeare's Hamlet.

That chimp really is a born actor, Darcy thought sadly. Then she shook her head. *But if I don't start thinking about my own acting, I'm gonna be as unemployed as the Baron is. Focus, Darce! Find your motivation.*

Putting her fingers to her temples, Darcy tried to shut everything out.

Superloaded 4x4, she told herself. *Extended cab pickup with seat warmers and a dozen cup holders. . . .*

Meanwhile, she became vaguely aware of a growing audience behind the camera! In addition to Victoria and Lindsay, Kathi and her dad had just arrived. The always-bubbly Kathi leaned down and tapped the director on the shoulder.

"I know her!" she blurted, pointing at Darcy.

"*I'm* still in charge, though, right?" the director quavered.

"Uh, yeah," Kathi said.

"Okay," the director said. Then he took a deep breath.

Wow, this dude is even more nervous than I am, Darcy thought.

"Everyone," the director called. "This is going to be a take. Roll camera, please. Are you ready, Darcy?"

This is it! My big moment!

Straightening her green cowboy hat one last time, Darcy glanced at Lindsay, who gave her an encouraging thumbs-up. Smiling gratefully, Darcy nodded at the director.

"And," the director said, *"action!"*

Darcy smiled into the camera, pumped her fist and cried, "Yeehaw! We're rounding up the bargains at Giraldi's Car Corral. We've got—"

"Eeeeee! Eeee! Eeeeee!"

Darcy stopped her spiel abruptly. That was the Baron! Despite Brett Brennan's efforts to keep him quiet, the chimp was jumping up and down next to the corn-dog cart, slapping at his head with his hands, and screaming like a banshee!

"Cut, please!" the director yelled.

Chapter 23

Wild Wisdom . . . *Monkeys differ from apes (such as chimpanzees) in that they have tails.*

At the director's order, Darcy planted her fists on her hips and scowled.

I was really feeling the drama of that moment, she complained to herself. *I was totally* one *with the used cars. And then the Baron had to go and ruin everything. What is his problem?*

The director had a question of his own.

"*What* is that noise?!" he demanded. "It sounds like a chimp screaming."

"It *is* a chimp screaming," Darcy said, pointing to the corn-dog cart, where Baron von Chimpie was still freaking.

"Well, okay then," the director said. "Uh, can someone do something about that?"

Brett and Brandon were way ahead of him. Brett

took the chimp's hand and led him to a director's chair on the far edge of the set.

"C'mon, Baron," Brett scolded. "If you can't behave, you have to sit over here."

Sadly, the chimp climbed into the chair.

"This isn't about you," Brandon said.

At this, the Baron slumped deep into his chair and put his hand over his eyes. Darcy felt a twinge in her belly. And since she'd totally lost her focus anyway, she took a minute to sidle up to Lindsay.

"Look at him," Darcy whispered to her bud as they both gazed at the despondent ape. "For a smelly, tomato-hucking devil-chimp, I really feel sorry for him."

"Darcy?" the director interrupted her. "We're ready to try again."

The show must go on, Darcy thought, shaking her head sorrowfully. She tromped back to her mark and looked into the camera. She tried to resummon her enthusiasm for all those slashed-price cars and trucks, but with the Baron exuding sorrow only a few feet away, it was hard!

"Camera's rolling," the director warned.

Remember, Darcy told herself. *You are a consummate professional. Don't think about the Baron now.*

Focus on the commercial . . . on your career . . . and definitely not *on the Baron, no matter* how *sad he seems.*

"And . . . action!"

Darcy took a deep breath and launched into her routine.

"Yeehaw," she said, weakly throwing out a couple cancan kicks. "We're rounding up . . ."

Suddenly, Darcy glanced at the Baron. She couldn't help it. It was like his slumpy, hairy little self was a magnet! Trying to shake it off, Darcy returned her gaze to the camera.

"Um . . ." she continued, "the bargains at . . . uh. . ."

Darcy couldn't help it. The Baron was too distracting. She just *couldn't* work under these conditions.

"And, cut!" she called out.

"Um," the director protested, "*I'm* supposed to say that."

"Yeah, can you give me, like, one *minute*?" Darcy spat. "Please?!"

As she hurried back over to Lindsay, Darcy overheard her mother bragging to the Brennan brothers: "She's starting to display a real knack for the diva part of this!"

That stopped Darcy cold.

Diva? she thought. *Wait a minute. If being a diva means dissing your friends and being mean to your director, maybe I need to rethink my career goals!*

Turning to the stung director, Darcy added, "You're doing a great job! Everyone's talking about it."

Then she grabbed Lindsay and took her aside for a quick heart-to-heart.

"You're right," Darcy admitted. "I *am* like the monkey. We've both been torn away from everything we love. But at least I've got great friends and everything to help me."

At this, Lindsay looked shyly at her feet. Darcy knew Lindsay liked sappy moments like this one about as much as she liked hugs, but Darcy couldn't help it. She wanted Lindsay to know that she wasn't going to take her for granted anymore.

And the same went for Baron von Chimpie.

"The least I can do for the Baron," Darcy declared, "is help *him* deal."

"You've already tried everything," Lindsay pointed out. "Need I remind you of the apple onslaught? The incident of the tractor? The assault on Eli?!"

"I haven't tried *everything*," Darcy said.

She marched up the Baron, who was still slumped

150

in his chair, depressed and dejected.

"Hey, Baron," Darcy offered. "Want to be in a commercial?"

Darcy held out her hand and flashed a welcoming smile at the chimp. Haltingly, the Baron took Darcy's hand and climbed down from the chair.

Darcy led the chimp onto the set. As she did, the Baron's sorrowful expression was replaced by one of glee! He lifted himself onto his hind legs, threw back his shoulders, and straightened the collar of his yellow polo shirt.

The Baron was back!

And Lindsay looked superimpressed. Darcy felt a warm glow in her gut as she sat down with the Baron to discuss motivation and choreography and such.

I guess the only thing that feels better than stardom, Darcy realized with a shrug, *is stardom shared!*

Chapter 24

Wild Wisdom . . . *Elephants are incapable of running and are the only animals that cannot jump.*

Darcy looked happily around her living room. It was hard to believe this was the same room that had recently endured the Baron's TPing, arrow-shooting, banana-hurling rampage.

A week after all that drama, the living room had been restored. The torn sofa cushions had been patched, the arrow dings had been buffed out of the walls, and all the toilet paper had been removed from the chandelier.

Darcy had even added a few new accessories. On the coffee table was a bowl brimming with hot popcorn. On the couch were her friends—Lindsay and Kathi. And on the television? It was Darcy's small-screen debut! Her commercial was just about to air!

While Kathi crunched on popcorn and Lindsay hit RECORD on the VCR, Darcy held her breath.

Suddenly, there she was! On TV! Her bright pink and green outfit looked fab, her smile was big and pearly white, and if Darcy did say so, her Texas accent was impeccable.

"Hi, I'm Darcy Fields for Giraldi's Car Corral," she drawled to the camera. "People ask how we can charge such low, low prices."

TV Darcy peeked over her shoulder and said, "Here's how—our sales manager is crazy. He's gone ape!"

With that, she walked a few steps to her left. When the camera followed her, it revealed . . . Baron von Chimpie! He was decked out in a pin-striped suit and sitting behind an executive's desk, looking very author-itative indeed. TV Darcy looked down at the Baron and announced, "We just got in a fully loaded pickup. I say we charge twenty thousand."

Splat!

Suddenly, TV Darcy's head was slammed with a cream pie! A cream pie thrown by none other than Baron von Chimpie.

Yup, Darcy thought with a giggle, *we really came up with a way for the Baron to put his pitching skills to use.*

He hit me right in the kisser with that one. Good thing coconut cream is my favorite flavor!

On TV, Darcy was smearing whipped cream out of her eyes and turning back to the Baron.

"How about fifteen thousand?" she proposed as a piece of graham-cracker crust fell off her cheek.

Splat!

Another cream pie landed on Darcy's face.

"How 'bout ten?" Darcy squeaked desperately. She threw her arms up to fend off another pie.

That pie never came, though. And when the camera swung on to the Baron, he was giving Darcy a thumbs-up and a big, chimpy grin.

Dripping in coconut cream by now, TV Darcy turned back to the camera.

"So come on down to Giraldi's Car Corral," she drawled, her voice slightly muffled by all the gunk on her face, "where you can make a monkey out of us!"

At that, yet another pie hit Darcy in the ear.

Splat!

And another!

Splat!

And yet a third!

That one, the Baron totally improvised, Darcy recalled as the commercial faded to black. *What a moment! He really is a natural actor. Now, I wonder what Lindsay and Kathi think of my performance.*

She looked at her buds expectantly.

Did they notice my subtle leaning toward a Paris, Texas, accent over a Dallas, Texas, one? Darcy wondered. *That was my little homage to Kathi! And what about my outfit? Did my wardrobe choices totally capture the vibe of Giraldi's Car Corral? And how did my hair and makeup look—*

"Well, you look ridiculous," Lindsay announced bluntly.

Harsh! Darcy thought. *Even if it is totally true. I mean, after the cream pies started coming.*

"But," Lindsay added quickly, "it was massively cool of you to do that for the Baron."

"Well," Darcy said with a smile, "the Baron needed a hand. I mean, animals are people, too."

She turned to Kathi.

"I'm sure Kathi's dad will make more commercials, someday," she said hopefully.

"Yeah, he plans to," Kathi said, a nervous smile on her face. Darcy couldn't help but notice that Kathi was wringing her hands nervously as well.

"But," Kathi went on to admit, "Dad only wants the chimp in them. Baron von Chimpie's going to stay with the Brennan brothers and be in all my dad's commercials."

"So, I lost my acting career to a monkey?" Darcy yelled. She threw herself back into the couch cushions indignantly.

I'm starting to really understand the Baron's rage! she thought. *Being an unemployed actor stinks! Much like a funky banana!*

"It's okay," Lindsay said with a sly smile. "You still have a job at Creature Comforts. In fact . . ."

Lindsay glanced at her watch.

" . . . there's still lots of stuff down there that needs to get done."

Great, Darcy sighed to herself. *Here I am, an unemployed actor and I don't even get the fringe benefits of unemployment! As in—freedom from work!*

On the other hand, Lindsay was counting on her. And to Darcy, that meant something.

"All right, all right, I get the hint," Darcy agreed, heaving herself off the couch. "Let's go. Let me grab a soda first."

As Lindsay and Kathi giggled at her—in the way that only true friends are allowed to—Darcy tromped into the kitchen. While she reached into the fridge and pulled out a can of something fizzy, she had to smile. *And* grab her laptop off the kitchen table.

❋ (DARCY'S DISH) ❋

Wow. My life has changed so much lately, my head
is spinning. I've gone from being the daughter of a
Hollywood star to being the daughter of a heartland
farm frau. Used to be, the closest I got to animals
was petting Paris Hilton's Chihuahua at movie premieres. Now I've got cows in my bedroom, spitting
llamas in my workplace, Chuck the Duck wandering
into the foyer, and an acting chimp stealing away
my dreams of stardom.

Darcy leaned against the kitchen counter and took
a swig of soda.

"Mraaaawwrrrrrrr!"

Darcy jumped away from her laptop and spit out
a mouthful of soda. That earsplitting trumpeting
sound, coming out of the yard—was that what she
thought it was?!

Plunking the soda can on the counter, Darcy ran
to the window. What she saw, just a few feet away
from her front porch, was so massive and so bizarre,
she could only take in parts of it at a time. She saw a
long, coiling trunk . . . whiskery legs that resembled
gray tree trunks . . . ears that flapped in the wind.

It *was* what Darcy had suspected—an elephant! An elephant, just hanging out in her yard, helping itself to some of those stinky tomatoes from the garden.

Maybe I should revise my "friend to all species" blog, Darcy thought frantically. *Let's say, "friend to all species of a thousand pounds or less!" So, when it comes to that tomato-chomping behemoth out there . . .*

Darcy turned from the window and yelled, "Mom! We're not babysitting for the Brennan brothers anymore! I mean it!"

DARCY'S DISH

Do you think she'll listen to me? I'm thinking—sure, until a really cute rhinoceros needs a little TLC. Oh, well. Life in Bailey can be a zoo, but, hey, what's more fun than a trip to the zoo, right . . .

All right, my people. I better go find some peanuts for our not-so-little visitor. Until I blog again, ciao from Barley! Whoops, I mean Bailey. Otherwise known as . . . home.